But At the End of the Day...
It's
king leo's
PRIDE

JOHN ANDERSON

To order additional copies of this book, contact:
Xlibris
844-714-8691
www.Xlibris.com
Orders@Xlibris.com

ISBN: Softcover   978-1-6641-5243-4
       Hardcover   978-1-6641-5244-1
       EBook   978-1-6641-5242-7

Library of Congress Control Number: 2021901548

Print information available on the last page

Rev. date: 01/30/2021

But at the End of the Day…It's King Leo's Pride

KING LEO

King Leo, *yawns*: As the rays from the morning sun touch my face, I'm embraced by the love of life and the dawn of a new day, a chance to test my strength and skills of life survival! Because my lady's light waits for no one. But she lets me knows that her love is always mine. And she welcomes me with open arms. Thanks, my love. I'm awakened by her warm kisses. It looks like a beautiful day today! (*He makes kissing sounds, then walks away. He looks at the cold black stone that looks like glass and starts climbing, kump kump kump.*) I remember not long ago, when I first tried to make this climb (*continues climbing, kump kump kump*), it was so hard for me then. My father, King Leo, always told me, in order to be a true king, I first must master this climb. I'll be king, and being king means that you have to be strong.

(*Continues climbing, kump kump kump*) Because only the strong survive and rule. (*Reaches the top of the pride rock*) I was faster than before (*laughs*).I surprise myself at times. (*He looks around with the wind blowing through his mane.*)

NARRATOR: As he gazes out, he overlooks the view of waterfalls falling from pink-and-yellow clouds with a hint of white as if they were magnolia leaves floating on a slow-moving stream. And the mist from the waterfalls creates drops of rain that falls on the meadows that disappear into the seven-foot running bamboo that stretches far as the eye can see. Hills and valleys are filled with green grass, plants, and flowers that dance from the sweet dew that's blown from the bamboo. And there's a tree. Not like any of the other trees. No! This particular tree is set in the middle of all the kingdoms that reach to the heavens. The sky is filled with creatures with wings that have vibrant colors, each one with different jewels and colors that when the sunlight hits them, they sparkle while humming sweet songs of love that fills the valley from end to end. In this valley all of the creatures inhabiting it live in one harmony.

KING LEO: It was many moons ago when my father told me, when the herds come feeding with their new young, it's the start of a new season, a season in which I'll be honored and embraced. Now that day has come for me to continue the respect of my father's pride. This day I will be king. My word, the word of my clan, hear my pride. I am King Leo (*roars, music sound effects play, etc.*).

NARRATOR: And the herds of the most extraordinary creatures, big and tall, some looking different from others' forearms and legs. With horns of different colors, short and small, with long strings of hair, by the twos, they come with their new offspring. They come to graze on the sweet green grass and drink from the marshlands of the bamboo and the nectar from the full-bloomed plants and flowers. Every tree is filled with life and songs of angels (*music and effects play, etc.*).

KINGU

KINGU looks up and yells, breaking Leo's thoughts.

KINGU: Leo, the herds are returning with their young.

LEO: So I see, Kingu. Round up everyone to welcome the herd and their young.

KINGU: *Yes*! Leo, will there be anything else?

LEO: Yes, that's King Leo.

KINGU: Not until the falling light. (*They laugh.*)

LEO: Wait, Kingu. Have the Sha'mush arrived yet?

KINGU: Not at the moment.

LEO: That's odd! Because there's never been a feeding before the Sha'mush arrives.

KINGU: A feeding—what are you talking about, Leo?

LEO: The herd is being attacked! (*Roars*)

KINGU: What? (*Roars*)

O'ANNES

O'ANNES and KISHAR come running.

O'ANNES: Troops! (*Roars*)

KISHAR: What's wrong, Kingu?

KINGU: The herds are being attacked.

O'ANNES: What shall we do, Leo, when the troops arrive?

LEO: We must hurry before he attacks their young. Kishar, stay here. (Jumps into battle formation.)

KISHAR: Who's he?

LEO: No time to explain. We must move now!

KINGU: Don't worry yourself, O'annes. Let's go!

LEO: Nishar! Like the wind save their young.

KISHAR: This is odd. I've never heard of anything like this in any season but, of all seasons, the one where Leo takes charge of things. Seems to me it's out of the ordinary. This is strange. I've…I've…I've never seen this. Something is wrong. I must go. (*She takes off running at the coming of the herds.*)

NI'NIB

NI'NIB: Who are you? You know it's forbidden to feed before the arrival of the Sha'mush, you cur!

AN'LB (a wolflike creature): Who are you to be questioning me? So I'm a cur! (*He then howls and charges towards NI'NIB.*)

NI'NIB: *Slash!*

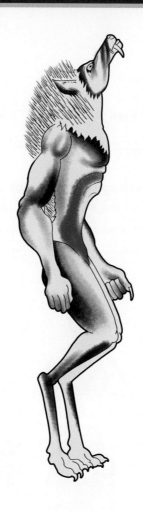

An'lb

An'lb: *Swoosh!*

Ni'nib: (*She steps back!*) *Slash! Slash!*

An'lb: *Swoosh! Swoosh!* (*He bites!*)

Ni'nib: (*She blocks, then kicks!*)

An'lb: (*Thinks to himself*) I see the Calvary coming. I must make haste.

Ni'nib: *Slash! Slash!*

An'lb: *Swoosh!* (*He bites.*) *Swoosh!*

Ni'nib takes a small hit, knocking her off-balance. Swoosh!

An'lb: I'm warning you, there will be a later! (*Howls and then takes off.*)

Ni'nib: Yes! There will be a later (*She gathers herself from the mistaken trip as Leo and the others reach her.*)

Leo: Ni'nib, are you all right?

Ni'nib: Yes! Leo, I'm fine. It's just a scratch.

O'annes: Who was that?

Ni'nib: That scoundrel didn't say who he was!

Kingu: That mutt!

Leo: Calm down, Kingu.

O'annes: That's right, Kingu. Get mad!

Leo: *Now* is not the time, O'annes.

Ni'nib: That's odd because this scent is unknown to me, as if it's just appeared from nowhere.

Kingu: That's not possible!

O'annes: You see, I see, but we don't see. You can't see me. You can't see me (*laughs*).

Ni'nib: (*Roars*) I'm going to put a leech on your face, O'annes. (*She begins to smile.*)

Leo: Wait! He's right. It's like magic. I want everyone to remember this scent.

Kingu: I have it, Leo.

Ni'nib: How can I forget it?

Leo: Remember this thing so the next time we get this scent, we will know who it is.

Up comes Kishar.

Kishar: What was it?

Leo: What are you doing here? I thought I told you to stay back.

O'annes: Leo, we must return to the herds.

Kingu: Ni'nib, here, let me help you.

Leo: Ni'nib, now tell me what happened between you two? (*Ni'nib explains.*)

Ni'nib: We fought, then he caught me with his claw, then he took off.

Kingu: That's not even possible.

NARRATOR: Kingu says this as he thinks to himself, *She's faster than Leo.*

O'ANNES: She was a tad bit slow this time. (*He starts laughing.*)

LEO: Let's get back and welcome the herds.

KISHAR: Leo, the Sha'mush should be here by now.

KINGU: That's good. Maybe they can put the light on this one.

O'ANNES: What light? That light? Oh, you talking about the dark light. (*Everyone starts laughing.*)

LEO: O'annes. (*He says this as he laughs.*)

NI'NIB: Leo, should we be on high alert?

LEO: No, just keep your eyes open. Agree? (*Everyone agrees as they begin to return back to the kingdom.*)

O'ANNES: Na na na na. Ni'nib's sword was just too slow. We should have known that her training is just too old. That's right, old, old, old.

KINGU: Don't start, O'annes.

NARRATOR: Nishar thinks to herself that that stench of the wolf is really unfamiliar. It's like he's been dead for many seasons, but yet it's something of an old, ancient clan.

Narrator: Meanwhile, there is the Bambaa Tu, a very unique race of monkeys that live in the mountains and hills of this vast land with borders of trees thicker than mulberry bushes, filled with hidden passages and trails (unbeknownst to the unfamiliar) surrounding this place of peace…or is it?

NINUR'TA

NINUR'TA (VO): I wonder where the prince is sneaking off to by the way of the forbidden.

Prince Zwolle looks around to see if anyone or anything is following him. He then turns and jumps (shift, shift, woosh, woosh, woosh) through the trees as he jumps from limb to limb. He stops (thump, shift, shift)! He looks both ways and slides down the hidden rock trenches. He lays flat to hear for any sound. Then he gets up and then jumps into the trees of the forest (woosh, woosh, woosh). He screams from the forest (scurry, scurry, womp, womp, swoo, swoo).

PRINCE ZWOLLE

PRINCE ZWOLLE (VO): That was too close. I stopped just in time.The shadows are really on the move early. I must stay on high alert coming back. (*He jumps, and then he stops, breathing heavy.*)

PRINCE A'NU: Ba'lar! You know I hate waiting. What's taking him so long to get here?

NARRATOR: Now Prince A'nu is the pride leader of the That-mus!

BA'LAR: My prince, he will be here, for he's the one who wishes to meet with you, sir.

PRINCE A'NU: This so-called prince wants to meet. Oh, he better hurry up before I change my mind because I don't have time for this, Ba'lar! I have other matters to attend to.

BA'LAR: Sir, he will be here. You have my word or my head.

PRINCE A'NU: Hmm, since you put it that way, your head will do just fine. Your head will be a reminder to all those who cross me.

Ba'lar: Sir, you don't have to be so frank about it.

Prince A'nu: Don't be so green about it. (*He laughs, and at that moment, there is a noise.*) What's that sound?

Ba'lar: It's coming from over there.

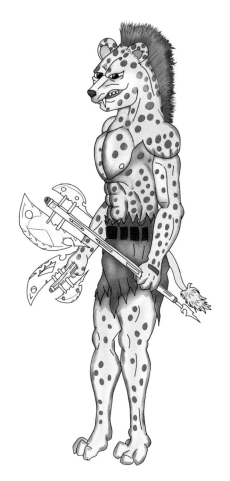

PRINCE A'NU

Prince A'nu: You two, go over there and see what's that noise.

Two of Prince A'nu's menacing soldiers darted into the darkness (pow, pow, klump, splush, pump, pow, swipe, swipe, pow, boom, bump, bam, klump, pow, kick, kick, boom, boom, boom, kick).

He slides the scoundrel at Prince A'nu's feet while dragging the other one by his arm and slamming him at the feet of Prince A'nu.

Prince Zwolle: I don't have time for these little shenanigans of yours, A'nu.

BA'LAR

Ba'lar lets out a sigh of relief.

BA'LAR: Prince Zwolle, so glad that you could make it.

PRINCE A'NU: What is the meaning of this?

PRINCE ZWOLLE: You send these little weaklings or whatever they are to attack me.

BA'LAR: Prince Zwolle, watch your mouth.

PRINCE A'NU: No, Ba'lar. He's right. They were weak to lose to an overgrown hair ball. Yes, weak, very weak
    indeed. (*He gives a slight, cocky chuckle.*)

PRINCE ZWOLLE: How dare you insult me!

PRINCE A'NU: Insult! No, not by any means, and also, let's not forget where you are, Zwolle.

BA'LAR: Please, sire, let's get on with this.

PRINCE ZWOLLE: You must be Prince A'nu.

PRINCE A'NU: Yes! That is I. (*He sticks his chest out proudly.*)

PRINCE ZWOLLE: Well, Prince A'nu, I'm here to offer you a chance to get revenge on those who did this to you and your father. You don't want back what they took? Look at your land. What do you have? I don't see any food running around here. (*He grins.*) I can help you, but only if you will join me in my quest to overthrow my father, and you can drink the blood of your enemies, (A'nu!)

Ba'lar gasps.

PRINCE A'NU: Now why would I do that, and what's in it for me?

PRINCE ZWOLLE: My father is getting old. It's time for a new *shaku* to rise up and lead the clan! And if you help me do this, in turn, you shall reap again for all which you have lost to me, and my army will be there to aid you in crushing Leo! (*He looks with eyes as black as coal.*)

PRINCE A'NU: I help you, and you help me, right? (*He giggles!*)

PRINCE ZWOLLE: Once I become *funji*, I will stretch your land to the forest, and you will have more than your belly's full.

PRINCE A'NU: To the forest!

PRINCE ZWOLLE: Yes! Which is more than you have now. You'll be able to feed more, more than you could ever imagine. (*He grins.*)

BA'LAR: Prince A'nu, sir! That sounds like a splendid offer, sir.

PRINCE A'NU: So it sounds good to you, Ba'lar?

BA'LAR: Yes, sir.

PRINCE A'NU: OK, Zwolle! I'll help you, but if I think for one moment that your peace of mind starts to put images in my mind, I will drink from your skull! (*He says this with hard giggles!*)

PRINCE ZWOLLE: Good then. But you must never come past the forest. Are we clear, A'nu?

PRINCE A'NU: Yes! Shaku.

BA'LAR: Do you know what this means, sir?

Prince A'nu replies with a very angry tone.

PRINCE A'NU: Quiet, Ba'lar!

PRINCE ZWOLLE: I like the way you rule, A'nu. So everythings is clear?

PRINCE A'NU: Yes.

PRINCE ZWOLLE: Good. Then we will meet again to execute my plan, A'nu, and in the meantime, get these lazy, unfit dogs into shape. Pathetic. (*looks at them shaking his head*)

PRINCE A'NU: Pathetic! (*A'nu giggles low, looking at Prince Zwolle as he turns to leave.*)

BA'LAR: My prince, what do you think of this offer?

PRINCE A'NU: Ba'lar, I love it, but I have a lot on my mind right now. So this discussion can wait until later. Let's go. And, Ba'lar…

BA'LAR: Sir!

PRINCE A'NU: Do something with them!

BA'LAR: Yes, sir!

He kicks and punches them as he laughs.

BA'LAR (VO): I've been wanting to eat you (*laughs*).

NARRATOR: Still at the That-mus, a small hair of tales tell of its journey!

HA'SAN: Where's Prince A'nu? (*He runs up to An'lb, the one who attacked the herds.*)

AN'LB: I don't know you, peasant! (*He says this as if he wants to eat him.*)

HA'SAN: Look who's talking, flea toter. (*He says this with a laugh as An'lb responded with a low growl.*)

AN'LB: Watch your mouth, silly varmint before you get eaten (*He slowly walks toward him.*)

HA'SAN

HA'SAN: Varmint? The little two-feet creature yells varmint, you dirty water drinker! (*He yells and runs at the kneecaps of An'lb.*)

AN'LB: Don't insult me, you little fool! (*Growls and chases after him.*) Varmint!

HA'SAN: Flea toter, I say! (*He coughs.*) You're going to pay for that. (*He pushes, kicks, punches, and swipes him!*)

AN'LB: That's enough of being nice. (*He growls and slashes and bites him.*)

PRINCE A'NU: What's that noise, Ba'lar?

BA'LAR: I don't know, sir, but it's coming from in there (*They walk over to Prince A'nu's chamber door.*)

PRINCE A'NU, *gasps in rage*: What is this? You two stop it right now. (*He punches An'lb and throws Ha'san out the window!*)

BA'LAR, *laughing quietly to himself*: This is an outrage.

AN'LB, *holding his growling stomach*: What did I do, sir?

BA'LAR: Looks like you made a mistake.

HA'SAN, *looks in the window*: Can't think. I can't think. (*He crawls back in.*)

PRINCE A'NU: Look at this mess! Who did this? Tell me now!

AN'LB: It was him, sir (*looks at Ha'san*).

HA'SAN: Surely not I, sir. (*He slowly gets himself off the floor.*)

PRINCE A'NU: Well! One of you better start talking!

AN'LB: It's Ha'san, sir. He did it.

PRINCE A'NU: Those are claw marks on my father's table! And bite marks on my thinking chair! And you expect me to believe that little Ha'san did this? (*At that very moment, Prince A'nu flashes a blow, sending An'lb flying.*)

HA'SAN: Ha ha ha!

PRINCE A'NU: You better have some good news for me because you will look very good on my feet. (*He giggles loudly.*)

HA'SAN: Si…Si…Sir, pl…pl…please, I know nothing about the Bambaa Tu clan

NARRATOR: For Ha'san is Prince A'nu little eyes and ears.

PRINCE A'NU: What? You telling me after this fool has been seen by one of them, you come back after being gone a whole season with *nothing*!

HA'SAN, *weeps*: I only know a little, sir.

BA'LAR: What? Tell us, what do you know of them?

HA'SAN: It's only a few of them that goes to the mountains, and Prince Zwolle is at war with his father. While his sister stared at the crab tree like she was crazy or something.

PRINCE A'NU: Look, you have until the second moon to bring me something, or I'll have a nice time walking on you (*giggles*). Now get out my face now!

HA'SAN: Right, sir (*turns and runs out*).

BA'LAR: Sir, clearly you didn't mean until the second moon?

PRINCE A'NU: I know what I said, Ba'lar.

BA'LAR: But, sir.

PRINCE A'NU: No buts. Leave me...Wait! Do you have something to tell me, An'lb?

NARRATOR: An'lb turns and tells the events that happened between him and an unlikely foe.

AN'LB: Yes! Everything went as planned, my lord.

PRINCE A'NU: Good. Good. I take it that you didn't harm any of their young. (*He giggles as if he did, so he can take his head off and use it as an armrest.*)

AN'LB: No! But I had a fight with one of their female warriors. She showed up as I was moving the herd.

PRINCE A'NU: What!

AN'LB: This female fighter showed up, and we fought, sir.

PRINCE A'NU, *giggles and walks toward An'lb*: I thought that I told you not to fight no one! Harm nothing, engage in no contact with no one is what I told you, An'lb!

AN'LB: But...but, sir, she attacked me first. What was I to do?

PRINCE A'NU: Run!

AN'LB: What? Run?

PRINCE A'NU, *giggles*: Those were your orders, and you disobeyed them—yet again.

AN'LB: But, Si—

PRINCE A'NU: But nothing! (*He punches An'lb, then throws him. flinging him like a ragdoll, sending him flying then sliding across the floor*) It's hard to find good help. (*He sits in his chair.*)

AN'LB: But, sir! I have this.

PRINCE A'NU: What is that, An'lb?

AN'LB: It's a piece of her rag (*hands the piece of clothing to Prince A'nu*).

PRINCE A'NU: The scent of a cat.

NARRATOR: He starts to think of his father and the best way to avenge his death. But how? And then it hits him.

BA'LAR: What are you thinking of?

PRINCE A'NU: Nothing! Ba'lar.

BA'LAR: What are you talking about, sir?

PRINCE A'NU: They will feel my wrath.

Ba'lar: That's not good.

Prince A'nu, *giggles*: This is a great day for me, Ba'lar.

Ba'lar: That's right, sir. (*He laughs along, with A'nu not knowing what he's thinking of.*)

Prince A'nu: That's right, Ba'lar. If that hairball of a *funji* comes back again. (*A'nu makes a hard giggle!*)

Ba'lar, *laughs along with Prince A'nu*: I couldn't have planned it better.

Prince A'nu: Ba'lar, our time is now!

Ba'lar: I wouldn't have it no other way (*They both begin to laugh*).

Narrator: Meanwhile, back at the pride, O'annes, still being his usual hilarious self, starts laughing.

O'annes laughs.

Ni'nib: Kingu? What's wrong with him?

Kingu: I don't know, and I'm afraid to ask.

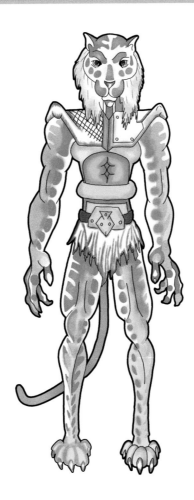

ELEVEN

ELEVEN: What is it, O'annes?

O'ANNES: Na na na na. Ni'nib's sword was just too slow. We should've known that her training was just too old. That's right, too old (*laughs*).

NI'NIB: All right, that's enough of the foolishness. En garde.

O'ANNES: Touch'e pussycat (*laughs*). Ting, ting, sling, swiff, ting, ting, ting.

NANNAR: Stop that, the both of you, before my father comes.

NI'NIB: He started it, so I'm gonna finish it…with his head.

KINGU: What? Are you mad?

O'ANNES: If a low-class wolf can land a hit on her, then so can I.

KI'SHAR: What was that you say? (*They keep fighting, ting ting, swipe, swipe, slash, swipe, ting, ting, swoop, swoop.*)

ELEVEN: Oh, I see now (*laughs*).

LEO, *roars*: Stop that fighting at once. What's the meaning of this?

NANNAR

NANNAR: They were just practicing, Father.

KINGU: Leo, they're just playing around.

NI'NIB: I'm going to kill this ant.

O'ANNES, *with a slight grimace*: Yeah! Like you did that wolf.

KI'SHAR: Leo, I must speak with you.

LEO: What's that you say, Ki'shar?

KI'SHAR: I must speak with you alone.

LEO: Fine. As you wish. Kingu.

KINGU: Yes, Leo?

LEO: Don't let things get out of hand in my absence.

KINGU: Yes, will do.

As Leo and Ki'shar walk to their chambers, Leo looks at Ki'shar and can see she's upset about something. They enter the chamber.

LEO: What's wrong, my love?

KI'SHAR: Leo, that scent I smelled earlier, that clan that I know with that scent is a peaceful clan, one I couldn't imagine doing something like this.

LEO: They? You mean there are more of these things?

KI'SHAR: Yes! I've been there.

LEO: You say they are a peaceful clan, but who is it that you a speak of

NARRATOR: Before she can say who they are, the sound of the horn goes off, letting them know that the Sha'mush has arrived. (*Horns blow.*) As everyone assembles in the meeting hall to see the guest, Leo knows he must tell the Sha'mush about the attack that happened.

SHA'MUSH: Come you all of the pride of Leo, come and hear the laws of this land and to obey them for the new season, for he or she that breaks the laws of this land will be put to death, (as everyone *gasps*)! Or casted out of these lands to live in the outters, where if seen in these lands after, the same death will come to you. I will now read the laws for this season! As it is written, there will be no hunting on the lands of the Bambaa Tu's! As it is written, there will be no hunting on the land of the That-mus, nor the land that no one is to speak of! As it is written, you are allowed to kill what you can catch, but no more than enough to feed the pack for a day, and what's left is for the scavengers. As it is written, the young will not be killed for this season, for this is the law....

ZEBIDIAH (THE SHA'MUSH KEEPERS)

LEO: Great Sha'mush, may I ask a question?

SHA'MUSH: Yes! What is your question, Leo.

LEO: Yes, has there ever been attacks before the laws were given?

SHA'MUSH: Yes Leo, it was long ago.

LEO: How long ago great Sha'mush?

SHA'MUSH: It was long before your father became king.

LEO: And what happened?

SHA'MUSH: War! And destruction of a clan that were more powerful as your own.

KI'SHAR: You mean!

SHA'MUSH: Yes! The name of the clan that can't be spoken of! Why do you ask this question, Leo?

LEO: I just wanted to know great Sha'mush.

SHA'MUSH: You're a bad liar Leo.

NI'NIB: Really great Sha'mush, Leo just wanted to know.

SHA'MUSH: You lie just as bad as he does. My child, come closer! (She walks over to him) Now tell me child, I smell a fresh cut, how did you get it?

NI'NIB: I was training great Sha'mush.

SHA'MUSH: You stink of lies child! What are you hiding? A little closer so I can see it better.

LEO: Wait! I'll tell you great Sha'mush, but only in my chambers will I tell you.

SHA'MUSH: Who are you to command the Sha'mush!?

LEO: Great Sha'mush, It is only a request.

SHA'MUSH: Very well Leo, I will hear you on your request.

LEO: Ni'nib and Kingu, take care of things here. Oannes Gaga prepare for tonight's hunt!

EVERYONE: Yes.

LEO: This way great Sha'mush. (*walking to his chamber*). Come, Ki'shar (*Leo tells her*). A set, great Sha'mush?

SHA'MUSH: Just one will do for the old one. This season is hard on him, but we young ones will take care of him. So now, Leo, tell us.

LEO: Right before you came, there were attacks on the herds and their young.

SHA'MUSH: (*Gasps!*) This is bad. This is very, very bad!

Then the Sha'mush started to speak in a language that Leo and Ki'shar couldn't understand.

KI'SHAR, *asking Leo as if he knew*: Do you know what they are talking about?

LEO: No, I thought that you did.

KI'SHAR: Funny, but whatever it is by the looks of it, it's not good.

SHA'MUSH: Hush, child! You don't know anything that you speak of!

LEO: Great Sha'mush, what is it?

SHA'MUSH: When the time is right, Leo, you will know everything. But until then, we must go now. The law of this land has been broken! (*They turn and leave.*)

LEO: Great Sha'mush, I will find out who did this!

SHA'MUSH, *walking out of Leo's chambers*: The law has been broken!

KI'SHAR: Leo, what do we do now?

LEO: We wait, but until then, we must hunt tonight.

KINSI KAAH: What are you two talking about?..

PRINCE A'NU: Nothing, my little friend...

BA'LAR: What shall we do now, my king?

PRINCE A'NU: Let's start part 2 of my plan.

KIN'SI KAAH: What's part 2?

PRINCE A'NU: It will be revealed soon...

BA'LAR: Shall I get the others, sire?

PRINCE A'NU: Yes, Ba'lar, by all means, do so...

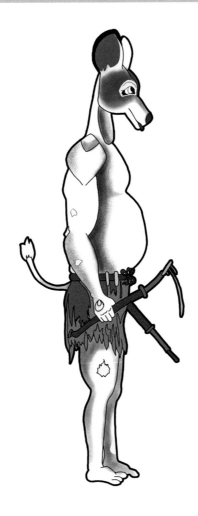

KIN'SI KAAH

KIN'SI KAAH: What's the big secret that you're hiding?

PRINCE A'NU: You'll find out in due time, Kin'si Kaah, so please sit...

KE'MET: You're so stupid, that you can't see that you're being used like an ant..

AN'LB: You're the one that's dumb, I don't know why you're here anyway..

KE'MET: What you don't know is that I'm better than you..

AN'LB: Ha! You're still licking dirt water (*laughing*)...

KE'MET: I'm not a curr...

AN'LB: Well, tell me this, how come every time there's a battle, you're late?..

KE'MET: 'Cause---...'cause, I'm the one who cleans up after you, you dog…!

An'lb: Watch your mouth, curr..!

Ke'met: Or what?!!

La hama: Will you two stop all this crying..?

KE'MET

Ke'met: He started it...

An'lb: You lying curr, just admit it...

La hama: Just stop it before Prince A'nu hears you both.

Ke'met: So what!

An'lb: I ain't scared of Prince A'nu.

La hama: You didn't say that earlier.

BA'LAR: When you girls get through kissing, the prince wants us all.

AN'LB: This isn't over, curr.

KE'MET, *as they approached the hall*: Not by a long shot.

PRINCE A'NU: Kin'si Kaah, what does this clan need?

KIN'SI KAAH: More hunting grounds..

PRINCE A'NU: That's right, and we shall have it..

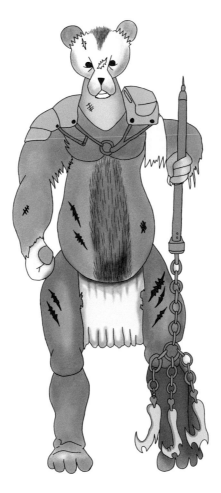

LA HAMA

LA HAMA: (Walking in) Have what?

PRINCE A'NU: Yes! The gang's here..

KE'MET: Yes, Prince A'nu, what are we here for?..

An'lb: Why have you… (*Grrrrr*)…

Prince A'nu: Glad you asked, now sit. For seasons, I've been trying to find a way to expand our land, and now is the time to do just that.

Kin'si Kaah: What are you talking about, sire?

Ba'lar: He's talking about us reaching the tree line!!

Prince A'nu: Ba'lar, please let me..

Ke'met: That's impossible, sire..

La hama: We haven't had much land since your father..

An'lb: Don't speak of his father.

Prince A'nu: He's right, An'lb, that land was ours when my father was alive, and with this new treaty with the ape, it will be ours again.

Ke'met: Can we trust him, sire?

Kin'si Kaah: The apes have a treaty with the pride, sire..

An'lb: Yes, the pride..

La hama: Those fleabags can't be trusted..

Prince A'nu: I know this about the ape, Prince Zwolle and that cat Leo…

Ke'met: Sire, if you think that this will work, I'm with you..

An'lb: Yes, you have my loyalty..

Kin'si Kaah: Sire? We live to look after our clan, of course I'm with you..

La hama: You've shown great strength with this move, Prince..

Prince A'nu: Fine, with that being said, rest up, for our time is now (*laughing*)…

Prince Zwolle: Ki'shargal, you know that Father is getting old.

Princess Ki'shargal: Yes, brother, and so is Mother.

Prince Zwolle: I will be the next Funji of this clan one of these lights soon, and I will rule better than my Father has.

Princess Ki'shargal: Oh, brother, you will be better than Father. I just wish I was strong just like our mother and rule beside my king one light! (*She smiles.*)

PRINCE ZWOLLE: My little sister, I know that you will always have my best interest at heart, but do you think that there's a good candidate who is worthy enough for you to take his hand, sister?

PRINCESS KI'SHARGAL: No, not yet. Why? Do you have someone in mind? (*She laughs...*)

PRINCE ZWOLLE, *smiling*: No, sister, I can't look for your king. You have to do it yourself, that's the only way!

PRINCESS KI'SHARGAL

PRINCESS KI'SHARGAL: Yes, you're right, brother. I'll just wait.

PRINCE ZWOLLE: Maybe that's best for now. Just wait and see what happens, OK, little sister.?

PRINCESS KI'SHARGAL: What are you talking about, Zwolle?

PRINCE ZWOLLE, *as he backs up*: I will be ruler of this land, and your so-called king will just have to wait!

PRINCESS KI'SHARGAL: What did you just say, Zwolle?! I don't have to wait. I have the same rights you have, Zwolle!

PRINCE ZWOLLE: My dear sister, you just don't get it, do you?!

PRINCESS KI'SHARGAL: Get what, Zwolle?

PRINCE ZWOLLE: That this is all about me, and your father and you have no place in this.

PRINCESS KI'SHARGAL: What are you saying, Zwolle?!

Prince Zwolle walks back up to her.

PRINCE ZWOLLE: THIS! (*He punches her in the stomach. She falls to her knees and looks at him.*)

PRINCESS KI'SHARGAL: It's been a long season brother.(*She jumps from the floor to the air and kicks Zwolle, which sends him flying backward. Booom!*)

PRINCE ZWOLLE: I see you've been training. That's good, so now I don't have to feel bad when I do this! (*Picking himself up, he rushes her. Kick, punch, punch, flip, flip, kick, kick.*) Show me what you got.

PRINCESS KI'SHARGAL: (*Blocks, blocks, kicks, ducks, sweeps, sweeps, kicks, punches. She flips two times after kicking him back, then she pulls her swords.*) Looks like you're getting old, brother.

PRINCE ZWOLLE, *standing back up*: You're Father's favorite, but that will end. This is my kingdom! (*He looks at her. He closes his eyes and opens them just before he attacks her with a move that she didn't see coming, and down she goes.*)

PRINCESS KI'SHARGAL: Why are you doing this, brother!

He picks her up and places her against the wall.

PRINCE ZWOLLE: Hear me, and you hear me good! If you think that you will rule this land with your king, trust me, little sister, I will kill every one of your kings. HEAR ME! (*She shakes her head to say yes.*) Good.

Prince Zwolle punches her one last time, and back to the floor she went, breathing hard as he walks away.

PRINCE A'NU: Ba'lar, you know the turning of the moon is almost here?

BA'LAR: Yes, sire! And what's your plan?

PRINCE A'NU: You know that you're my trusted friend and wise counsel.

BA'LAR: Yes, sire!

PRINCE A'NU: This is what I must share with you. My master plan, my friend, of the upcoming event that's about to happen.

BA'LAR: What are you talking about, sire?

PRINCE A'NU: The death of Prince Zwolle!..

BA'LAR: The death of who?.. Sire, you can't be serious.. (*with a look of disbelief*).

PRINCE A'NU: Yes, my friend, I am...

BA'LAR: Sire, that will cause a war between us and Lord Nunu..

PRINCE A'NU: You're right about one thing. Yes, it will be a war, but not with us..

BA'LAR: What do you mean? That it won't be our fight?

PRINCE A'NU: I will kill Zwolle and blame it on the pride and seek a treaty with the Bambaa Tu's and stretch our land farther than what Zwolle is willing to give us..

BA'LAR (*Still looking astonished*).

PRINCE A'NU: (*Easy*) The next time he comes to see us and finalize our deal, he'll never leave...

BA'LAR: We can't do this...

PRINCE A'NU, *Crash—throwing things around*: I'm tired of us living like foul beas...! (*Crash—throws more things around*) And the rest of those kingdoms are living in harmony (*crash*). Not this time (*crash*). We will live just like the rest of them (*crash*). We deserve to be treated with respect, (*crash*) and respect we will have (*crash*)...

BA'LAR: Sire, calm down, you know what happens when you go off into a rage..

PRINCE A'NU: Yes, Ba'lar, you're right..

BA'LAR: Save all your anger until the time is right, sire. The day will come when you will be able to unleash that which you've been holding on to for so long, sire...

PRINCE A'NU: I guess you're right, Ba'lar.

NEF'FA, *walking in*: What's all this noise?

A'LAM

A'LAM: Sounds like Prince A'nu, my queen..

MA'TIM: Shall I go knock him out, my queen?

MA'TIM

Tu'mur: Yes! Yes! Knock him out, knock him out!

Nef'fa: Hahaha. No, Ma'tim, let him be for now...

LA'LU

LA'LU: No!!

NEF'FA: What's wrong, La'lu?

LA'LU: Queen, he needs his tailbone broke..

LAHMA Tell me about it, Queen, please let me break it...

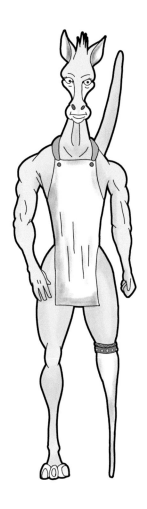

LAHMA

NEF'FA: No, no, no. It's good for him to let it all out.

(As they all turn to leave, Prince A'nu just looks at them)..

BA'LAR: My prince..

PRINCE A'NU: What, Ba'lar?

BA'LAR: Why did you do that, sire?

PRINCE A'NU: I needed to know where they were..

BA'LAR: My prince, you will be a true king...

PRINCE A'NU: I know *(laughing)*.

Queen Gu'det Screaming as lord Nunu rushes in.

LORD NUNU: What's wrong, my love! (*Looks around the room to see if anyone else is there, with his sword in hand and the twins behind him.*)

QUEEN GU'DET: There's no intruder in here. I just got a bad feeling.

QUEEN GU'DET

LORD NUNU: What's wrong, my love? (*He begins to hug her.*)

QUEEN GU'DET: Oh it's awful!

With her head on his chest crying, Ninur'ta, Na'bu, and Mar'duk comes running in.

MAR'DUK: What's wrong, my lord!?

NA'BU: Ancient monkey talk!

NINUR'TA: Is everything all right, sir?

QUEEN GU'DET: No, it's not all right!

LORD NUNU: Twins guard the door!

LORD NUNU

TWINS: Yes, my lord.

ISH'KAR & AN'SHAR (TWINS)

QUEEN GU'DET: It's awful, just awful. He's free (*she screams*)!

LORD NUNU: Who's free!?

QUEEN GU'DET: Him, he's free!..

NA'BU: Ancient monkey talk!

MAR'DUK: That can't be. Say it isn't so, my queen!

MAR'DUK

LORD NUNU: My queen, calm yourself. There's no way he's free. Calm down.

NINUR'TA: My queen, he's locked away very tightly within the mountains.

LORD NUNU: Yes! You see, there's nothing to worry about, love.

QUEEN GU'DET: No! I saw him free from that place, running around freely and killing! (*She cries in his chest.*)

LORD NUNU: My love (*as he holds her*), please calm yourself now. You're talking nonsense. There's no way he's free. Ninhar'sag and Ma'sha would have notified us.

QUEEN GU'DET: You don't understand, I saw him break free. Oh! It's awful, very awful. I fear that there's something coming for us all, my love.

NA'BU: Ancient monkey talk!

NINUR'TA: Hush, Na'bu! My queen, I've been feeling the same way myself, but I know for certain that he's still there, my queen. Just on the last night of the moon, I went there myself, and everything was fine.

NA'BU: Low growl!!

NA'BU

Lord Nunu: See, my queen, there's nothing to worry about (*as he holds her*).

Queen Gu'det: I'm sorry to have scared you, my love.

Lord Nunu: No, my dear, it's not a problem. You just need some rest. All you need is rest, okay..

Queen Gu'det: You're right, maybe that's what I need is some rest. Okay, I'm fine now, and you all can leave please.

Lord Nunu: Get some rest, my dear.

With this said, Lord Nunu kisses her and they all began to leave, but Lord Nunu is a little disturbed about what just happened with his wife.

Lord Nunu: Twins, come, I have a mission for you two.

An'shar: Yes, my lord.

Ish'kur: A mission, you say?.

Lord Nunu: Shhh! I don't want the queen to hear you. Na'bu, go through the land and see what you can find out about this.

E'nama: My lord, what shall I do?

E'NAMA

Lord Nunu: Listen, Ninur'ta, you go with Enama and see if my kingdom is guarded well. Nunu and twin, when you do go, go one at a time to the mountains to see if there's anything wrong. Mar'duk, you come with me.

Everyone: Yes!!

Lord Nunu: Please go now, and be discreet about how you go about this. We don't want to alarm the clan, but by all means, please be careful and report to me if anything is out of the ordinary... Now, go!

Prince A'nu: Inform the rest I have a mission..

Ba'lar: Yes, sire!

Prince A'nu: And tell them to be quiet about this mission!

Ba'lar: Yes, sire!

Prince A'nu: No, Ba'lar, forget it..

Ba'lar: Why, sire?

Prince A'nu: We wait..

Ba'lar: We wait, sire?

Prince A'nu: Everything will come to us (*laugh*ing).

Lord Nunu: Zwolle, I've been looking for you. We need to talk, my son...

Prince Zwolle: About what, Father?

Lord Nunu: About your actions lately .

Prince Zwolle: I don't want to hear this.

Lord Nunu: Well, you're going to, like it or not, but you will listen to me..

Prince Zwolle gives a low growl, looking at his father, with kill in his eyes..

Lord Nunu: Whenever you're ready, just say the word, or otherwise, sit down..

Prince Zwolle: Yes, Father (*sighs*)..

Lord Nunu: My son, you know the season is coming for you to lead this tribe. But you haven't yet chosen a wife and shown leadership skills..

Prince Zwolle: What do you know, Father?

Lord Nunu: No true king has ever ruled without a wife by his side, my son.

Prince Zwolle: Would it make you feel better if I said I have chosen a wife?

Lord Nunu: Oh yeah! Who's the lucky chimp?

Deep down in the forest...

Announcer: Please, please, place your bets now..

HARN (THE ANNOUNCER)

The crowd cheers on and talks loudly...

ANNOUNCER: Now coming to the ring is the undefeated champion An'kij.

The crowd sighs as they watch An'kij walk to the ring..

ANNOUNCER: Now coming to the ring is the two-time winner, the silverback gorilla Unslaw!!

The crowd erupts in cheer and praise at the favored one of the fight..

ANNOUNCER: This is the last stand, so the bets are in. Now ring the bell... (*Ding, ding, ding!*)..

UNSLAW *hums…hums…sweeps, kicks, hums, hums, strikes.*

UNSLAW

An'kij blocks, blocks, flips, blocks, blocks, flips.

ANNOUNCER: What an amazing show of strength by Unslaw, using his power first. But his power isn't phasing An'kij..

An'kij jumps, kicks, strikes, strikes, strikes, kicks, sweeps, pow, pow, throws, slams.

UNSLAW: Uuuurrrlllll!

ANNOUNCER: The champ is showing amazing quickness with his feet, and he's releasing a super combo on Unslaw!

An'kij flips, flips ninja style, does a handstand, and power kicks Unslaw with a fury of legs—kicks, kicks, swoops, swoops, kicks. Now spinning—whoo, whoo, whoo, bounces, stomps, stomps, kicks, stomps, kicks..

UNSLAW: Oh, oh, aah, oh, ooh, aaahhh!

Ump, ump, um, um, um—uuuurrrrlllll! (*Slides, roars, whuup, whuup, boom, boom, boom, charges, charges, swings, swings, shoulder swings, sweeps, kicks, punches, punches, kicks!*)

AN'KIJ *ducks, ump, pow, flips, blocks, blocks, catches, catches, monkey-flips and jumps with a knee.*

UN'SLAW *miss, rolls, sweeps, sweeps, flips, slashes.*

An'kij hums, sweeps, slams, cranes, stands, slaps.

AN'KIJ

UN'SLAW: Drunken gorilla style! (*Wobbly, wobbly, double wobbly, one-hand stand, punches, kicks, kicks! Punches, kicks, flips, spins, kicks. Wobbly, wobbly, backhands, spinning uppercut. Wobbly wobbly!*)

And with that fury of blows landing hit after hit, An'kij backs him up, making him cough up blood! But An'kij smiles.

AN'KIJ: The drunken crane style? Along with the drunken chimp style. Let's see if we can't put a stop to this right now! (*Sways, sways, claps, claps, rolls, head-butt, flips, punches, kicks! Spins, kicks, sways back, slaps double slaps, kicks kicks kicks! Rolls, punches, heart punches, bear hugs, rolls flips knee to the sternum, bounces, bounces, double knees, punches, punches and throws.*)

ANNOUNCER: Looks like that last attack hurt Un'slaw really bad!

UN'SLAW, *barely stands*: Please, no more!

AN'KIJ: Do you forfeit?

UN'SLAW, *pants and clenches his teeth tightly*: Please no more!

AN'KIJ: Do you give up? (*walks up close to Un'slaw, but Un'slaw catches him by surprise!*)

Un'slaw rapidly punches! Pow pow pow pow pow pow pow power punch! Boom boom, causing An'kij to slide back.

AN'KIJ: Ha ha ha! Good one, now it's time!

FA'HISH jumps up and down, does ancient monkey talk.

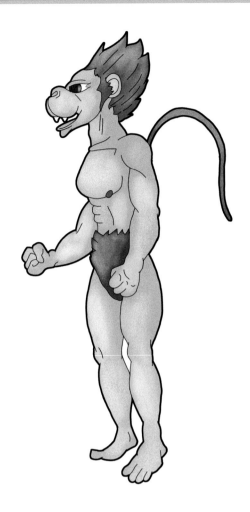

FA'HISH

AN'KIJ: I'm going to bury your corpse!

UN'SLAW: Yeah, right! I'm going to chop you in half!

AN'KIJ: What do you have?

UN'SLAW: My pet and everything I've won! I'm making this a death match.

AN'KIJ: Indeed, do you want to be free?

Fa'hish ancient monkey talks, jumping up and down at An'kij.

AN'KIJ: Okay then, you're on.

ANNOUNCER: All right, chimps and chimpness, this is now a fight to the death! Our champion hasn't been challenged to a death fight in five seasons! Will we crown a new champion or bury a fool? So place your bets now!

UN'NI: He looks so brave out there.

TIAMAT: Hmm (*walks away*).

UN'NI: I just love the way he fights, Tiamat.

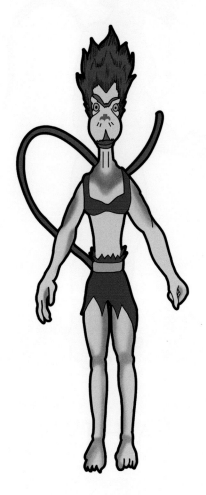

UN'NI

ANNOUNCER: OK, choose your weapon!

Un'slaw, *picks up a sword*: Now you will pay!

AN'KIJ: As you wish (*swings, swings, slashes, round steps, strikes, punches, swipes, swipes, ducks, Bob and weave, punches, overhead chops, dodges, strikes, strikes, strikes*) Urggh!

TIAMAT, *yells*: An'kij! Stop playing with your toys!

FA'HISH does ancient monkey talk.

AN'KIJ: Fine!

Un'slaw: You will die!

An'kij: OK then, kung fu strike! (*Swings, swings, swings, punches!*)

He doesn't see it coming.

Un'slaw, *gasps and falls*: You win. You win.

Announcer: What an amazing move! Un'slaw is down folks, and it looks like he's not getting back up any time soon! An'kij is still champion!

Crowd: An'kij! An'kij! An'kij!

An'kij walks out of the ring and looks back.

Un'slaw: Wait, wait! I see that you're the best fighter there is. I'll come with you now, friend of Un'slaw.

An'kij: Yes, friend, we have a lot of work to do (*smiles*).

Tiamat: I don't know why you come here instead of training.

TIAMAT

AN'KIJ: This is training, Mother.

TIAMAT: No, it's not! Now let's leave.

An'kij sighs and walks off.

TIAMAT: What, An'kij? What are you going to do with this thing?

AN'KIJ: I don't care! Give it away.

TIAMAT: To whom?

AN'KIJ: Give it to her!

Fa'hish does ancient monkey talk.

TIAMAT: Who?

AN'KIJ: To her right there (*points at Un'ni, the princess's eyes and ears, not knowing who she is*). She comes to all my fights. Give it to her.

Fa'hish does ancient monkey talk and bows!

AN'KIJ: You go with her now. You're free.

Fa'hish does ancient monkey talk.

AN'KIJ: All right, I order you to go with her.

TIAMAT: You come here.

UN'NI: Who, me?

TIAMAT: This gift came from that fighter. He wants you to have it.

UN'NI: Oh! Thanks, but what shall I do with it?

Fa'hish does ancient monkey talk.

UN'NI: What did he just say?

TIAMAT: It's yours to do whatever you want to do with it (*walks off*).

UN'NI: Well, I guess.

Fa'hish does ancient monkey talk.

UN'NI: I can't understand you, so shut up!

Fa'hish does ancient monkey talk and sticks out his tongue.

Now after just watching the fight between An'kij and Un'slaw, Na'bu leaves, talking to himself.

NA'BU: That was a good fight. I feel like fighting now! I must relieve myself (*flips using his feet to grab a rock and throws it*).

NI'JIM: Who did that? Who just hit me with this rock?

NA'BU (VO): It must be my lucky day.

NI'JIM: You there! (*Na'bu gasps*) It's you?

Na'bu does ancient monkey talk.

NI'JIM: I've been looking for you.

Na'bu does ancient monkey talk.

Ni'jim: Father wants you to come home.

Na'bu does ancient monkey talk.

Ni'jim: Yes, he does! And you're coming with me, Na'bu!

Ni'jim

Na'bu: Um, um.

Ni'jim: Yes, you are!

Na'bu does ancient monkey talk.

Ni'jim: If that's the way you want it, Na'bu!

Na'bu pows, punches, kicks, sweeps!

Ni'jim (VO): He's stronger now.

Na'bu stops and smiles.

NI'JIM: I'm not here to fight with you, so don't push your luck, Na'bu! (VO) He's stronger now. I can't beat him. Something is wrong.

Na'bu does ancient monkey talk.

NI'JIM: I agree, no weapons. (VO) I can't beat him.

Na'bu does ancient monkey talk.

NI'JIM: Yes, I'm ready, Na'bu!

Na'bu does ancient monkey talk, but before Ni'jim can blink, Na'bu attacks him. Kicks, punches, flips, kicks, kicks, counterpunches, counter-kicks, swoops, sweeps, double flips, flips, kicks with a ten-punch combo, slips, slips, three-piece combo, kicks, grapple throw stance, attack for attack!

Ni'jim flips, flips, somersaults into the air, and hangs from the roof with his tail!

Na'bu does ancient monkey talk.

NI'JIM: I told you, Na'bu! I didn't come here to fight with you.

Na'bu does ancient monkey talk.

NI'JIM: You still haven't changed, Na'bu!

Na'bu does ancient monkey talk.

NI'JIM: No, I'm not a coward, Na'bu. Your father will be angry when he finds out about this!

Na'bu does ancient monkey talk.

NI'JIM: Don't give me that, Na'bu! You refuse to listen. Now Father sent me to come get you and bring you back home. But all you want to do is fight!

Na'bu does ancient monkey talk.

NI'JIM: No! I will not continue with this!

Na'bu does ancient monkey talk.

NI'JIM: When that light comes, but not until then.

Na'bu does ancient monkey talk.

NI'JIM: I'm not a coward. You are!

Na'bu screams. That makes him mad, very angry. That's when Ni'jim knows that it is time to go. (He swings by his tail, and over the rooftop he goes. Na'bu chases after him, screaming, but can't find him. He disappears, not knowing why he is so enraged. He lands on one of the pride's outpost.

GUARD 1: Who goes there?

GUARD 2: What's that?

GUARD 3: It's an ape! What are you doing here? You know the law?

ZAAM'TU (LORD NUNU'S GUARD)

Na'bu does ancient monkey talk.

GUARD 1: You're trespassing on pride land!

Na'bu does ancient monkey talk and shakes his head.

GUARD 2: You will die for trespassing, ape!

Na'bu looks at the guards and smiles, then draws his swords.

Guard 3 swings at Na'bu!

Ni'nib blocks, cling, cling, swoosh, swoosh, cling, and kills him.

GUARD 1: He just killed him! Attack!

Guard 2 roars! The rest of the guards came running, while Ni'jim watches in a nearby tree.

NI'JIM: He'll never learn.

Na'bu looks around and sees he's surrounded and goes into his ancient fight stance with a sinister smile on his face.

GUARD 1: Charge! (*Cling, cling, swoop, cling, cling, cut, urrgh, cling, cling, uuull, punch, kick, flip, flip, slash, cut, slash, cut, kick, ump, uuhhh, punch, slash, power punch. One of the guards slips off with only a few broken ribs into the forest.*)

NI'JIM: I see now how powerful you've become, Na'bu! You've become stronger than I. I must tell Father about this (*disappears into the trees*).

Na'bu does ancient monkey talk and points at one guard.

GUARD 1: You're on pride land. You have committed murder treason. Now face death (*surrounds him*).

Na'bu does ancient monkey talk.

GUARD 1, *tells the others*: If you can stand a chance in melee war, then you might be allowed to leave, but to never return if you so choose. Choose now!

GUARD 2, *roars*: I will stay. We will all stay.

Na'bu humps and laughs sinisterly. Punch, kick, kick, punch, swing, duck, swing, pow, bam, slap kick, kick, sweep, punch, punch, kick, flip, strike, strike, urrgh! Slap, bump, slip, slash, and break, crunch, kick, punch, urrrgh. Ump, ump, break, leaving them all dead. He jumps back into the darkness of the trees laughing.

LEO: Ki'shar, you said that it's something that you wanted to talk about?

PRINCESS KI'SHAR

PRINCESS KI'SHAR: Oh, yes, my love. It's very important that I have a word with you. There's this clan that I used to play with when I was young.

LEO: Why haven't I heard of this before, my love?

PRINCESS KI'SHAR: It's been many moons since I've seen one of their clan.

LEO: What clan?

Before she could tell him, Queen Fa'tima bursts in (boom!).

QUEEN FA'TIMA: Leo! My son, I must speak with you now!

LEO: Mother, is there something wrong?

QUEEN FA'TIMA: You, uh! Ki'shar, can I have a word with my son alone, please?

Princess Ki'shar: Yes, Your Majesty. (*She looks at Leo before leaving.*)

Leo: Mother, what's the meaning of this?

Queen Fa'tima: The meaning of this, my son, is that it's time for you to leave and take your journey, just like the kings before you my son. This bloodline has never been broken, and it won't!

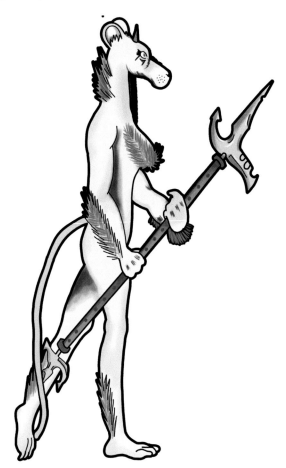

Queen Fa'tima

Leo: What do you mean, Mother, a journey! (*low ggggrrrr*)

Queen Fa'tima: See, that's what I mean right there, my son.

Leo: Mother! I don't have time for this.

Queen Fa'tima: My son, there was a time that your father, like yourself, had this great urge in him, and when this urge came, he found a way to control it.

Leo: I don't understand, Mother.

QUEEN FA'TIMA: And you will never, unless you go to the Valley of the Kings and speak with your father, my son.

LEO: My father! What can he tell me, Mother, that you can't? He's in the spirit world.

QUEEN FA'TIMA: You'll just have to trust me. And, son, be safe because this is a journey that'll test your strength and willpower all at the same time.

LEO: Father once told me that only a few have returned from the Valley of the Kings, and you want me to go there, Mother?

QUEEN FA'TIMA: You must go, my son, for only you can fulfill your destiny. Go to your father and learn your way.

LEO: Mother, please!

QUEEN FA'TIMA: Hush now! Go prepare yourself for your journey, and son…

LEO: Yes, Mother.

QUEEN FA'TIMA: Be strong, my son (*she walks away*).

NI'NIB: I have to get out of here and clear my mind.

PRINCESS KI'SHAR: Ni'nib! Where are you going?

NI'NIB: To get some fresh air. It's stuffy in here.

PRINCESS KI'SHAR: Oh! Please be careful.

NI'NIB: I will, and please don't tell Leo that I've left.

PRINCESS KI'SHAR: I won't. Just be careful out there.

NI'NIB: Will do.

KINGU: O'annes, all this talk about being ready for war or battle has a lot of us on edge.

O'ANNES: You're right, Kingu, and I, for one, could use a little rest.

KINGU: Who are you telling? Look, O'annes, tell the troops to be on alert.

O'ANNES: And Leo?

KINGU: I'll take care of it Leo. Just give out the order.

O'ANNES: Okay, will do.

LEO: Kingu, how are the troops looking? (*As he walks up*)

KINGU: Just look for yourself! (*As they watch the troops practice*)

LEO: They look fine. Make sure they're rested. Some of them look tired.

KINGU: Yes, Leo, will do. Is there anything else?

LEO: Yes! And make sure that you rest yourself.

KINGU: Will do. (*As they both laugh!*)

VOICE: I see that your powers have grown.

NIN'SISHZIDDA: Who are you?

NIN'SISHZIDDA

VOICE: It is I, the one who made you what you are!

NIN'SISHZIDDA: This is not real!

VOICE: Yes! I'm real.

NIN'SISHZIDDA: Stop talking to me!

VOICE: You stop talking to me!

NIN'SISHZIDDA: What do you want?

VOICE: War! war, war, war.

NIN'SISHZIDDA: We did that once before, didn't we?

VOICE: Yes, so long ago, and who put you in here? Say it!

NIN'SISHZIDDA: My brother Nunu! He's the one.

VOICE: Yes! And he will pay for what he did to us!

NIN'SISHZIDDA: Yes! He must pay for putting me in this place!

VOICE: We are stronger than before, more powerful than ever!

NIN'SISHZIDDA: Yes, more powerful than ever!

VOICE: They will all die! Hahahaha!

NIN'SISHZIDDA: Yes, they will! (*makes a low growl*)

NI'JIM: Father.

HA'KIM: Yes, Ni'jim

NI'JIM: I found Na'bu.

HA'KIM: Did he agree to come home?

NI'JIM: No! Father, he refused to come. And, father?

HA'KIM: Yes.

NI'JIM: We fought, Father. Na'bu has gotten stronger. He's powerful.

HA'KIM: So he's not coming back?

NI'JIM: No, Father.

HA'KIM (VO): My son.

PRINCE A'NU: Ba'lar! It's time for us to go with my plan and kill Zwolle.

BA'LAR: Everything is ready, sir.

PRINCE A'NU: Good. Then the second moon is almost among us.

BA'LAR: That's true, sir. What about your informant? Is he to be trusted?

PRINCE A'NU: Who cares! As long as he has the information that I need.

BA'LAR: True, sir. I was just wondering.

PRINCE A'NU: Ba'lar! Stop your sniveling and get on with it. I have no time for this in my home, our home. Understand?

BA'LAR: But, sir.

PRINCE A'NU: No buts! Just do it.

BA'LAR, *sighs*: Yes!

PRINCESS KI'SHARGAL: Un'ni! I'm so glad to see you. (*As she runs up to her friend in the palace halls, hugging her*).

UN'NI: What's wrong, Ki'shargal?

PRINCESS KI'SHARGAL: It's Zwolle. He's out of control!

UN'NI: What do you mean?

PRINCESS KI'SHARGAL: He's lost his mind!

UN'NI: You must tell your father about this.

PRINCESS KI'SHARGAL: I can't, Un'ni! That means I would have to break the royal rule.

UN'NI: So you're not going to tell him?

PRINCESS KI'SHARGAL: No, I can't wait! Who is this?

UN'NI: My little bodyguard (*smiles*).

PRINCESS KI'SHARGAL: Your what? (*makes a friendly laugh*)

UN'NI: My bodyguard (*smiles*).

PRINCESS KI'SHARGAL: Where did you get him from?

UN'NI: He was a gift from this fighter. Wait! You're not going to get off the hook so easily! So what happened with you and Zwolle? (*folds her arms!*)

PRINCESS KI'SHARGAL, *with a sad look now upon her face*: I don't want to talk about it.

UN'NI: Girl, spit it out?

Fa'hish does ancient monkey talk.

UN'NI: Shhh! I can't understand a word you're saying!

PRINCESS KI'SHARGAL: If you were paying attention in class, you would know that he's speaking the old tongue.

UN'NI: History has always been boring to me. And you're still avoiding the question.

PRINCESS KI'SHARGAL, *sighs*: All right, but it doesn't leave this room!

Fa'hish does ancient monkey talk!

UN'NI: I don't talk like that.

PRINCESS KI'SHARGAL: Speaking truthfully. I like him Un'ni (*smiles*).

UN'NI: That will be the first (*rolls her eyes*).

PRINCESS KI'SHARGAL: Tsk, tsk (*laughs*).

UN'NI: Stop teasing me, you crude (*laughs*).

PRINCESS KI'SHARGAL: Okay, Okay. Listen, my brother Zwolle is up to something. I think he's going to kill our father!

UN'NI: But why?

PRINCESS KI'SHARGAL: Because he knows that I'm going to fight him for the throne. Plus I've been seeing him going through the forbidden trail, and Un'ni, we had an open melee.

UN'NI, *gasps*: Why!

PRINCESS KI'SHARGAL: I needed to know if I could beat him, and I can.

UN'NI: Well, I wouldn't be your best friend if I didn't say let's have some fun. So what do we do?

PRINCESS KI'SHARGAL: We're going to wait until the time is right.

UN'NI: Why wait when we can get him now?

PRINCESS KI'SHARGAL: As long as he thinks that he can beat me, then I'm not a threat to him.

UN'NI: Oh, I see now.

PRINCESS KI'SHARGAL: Now did you see him?

UN'NI: Him who?

PRINCESS KI'SHARGAL: Stop joking around (*pushes her friend in a friendly way*).

UN'NI, *laughs*: Yes, I did. He had a fight.

PRINCESS KI'SHARGAL: Oh! What happened?

UN'NI: He beat him.

PRINCESS KI'SHARGAL: Oh! I wish that I was there to see him.

Fa'hish does angry wild monkey talk.

PRINCESS KI'SHARGAL: It's Okay, Fa'hish.

UN'NI: He's yours, from him.

PRINCESS KI'SHARGAL: Really?

UN'NI: Yes, really (*as she looks at Fa'hish*). By the sword of your new master, I give you to Princess Ki'shargal to protect her for the rest of your life.

Fa'hish does wild monkey talk.

LEO: Ki'shar, I must speak with you before I go to the Valley of the Kings.

PRINCESS KI'SHARGAL: Yes, Leo, I must speak with you as well.

LEO: Go on, my love.

PRINCESS KI'SHARGAL: That scent is from a very old race. They call them the Askia.

LEO: The what?

PRINCESS KI'SHARGAL: The Askia. They are a race of wolves that used to be on our land quite some seasons ago, but that was when I was a cub.

LEO: So what happened to them?

PRINCESS KI'SHARGAL: Exile! But for what, I don't know. You'll have to ask your mother, for only she and your father know why they were exiled.

LEO: Why are you just now telling me this?

PRINCESS KI'SHARGAL: I tried to tell you earlier, but your mother interrupted us, and your anger scared me.

LEO: I'm sorry, Ki'Shargal! That's why I must go to the Valley of the Kings.

PRINCESS KI'SHARGAL: Please be careful, Leo. You know how you get when your temper gets the best of you.

LEO: I know, my love. But while I'm gone, make sure that all is well here.

PRINCESS KI'SHARGAL: I will, my future king.

They hug each other, and then he was off. Meanwhile, Ni'nib is dealing with problems of her own.

KINGU: My queen, may I ask you something?

QUEEN FA'TIMA: Yes, you may, Kingu.

KINGU: How was King Lee? I know he was a great king, plus I hear so many tales about him—the battles, the wars!

QUEEN FA'TIMA: That's true, Kingu, my child. (*As she thinks back to the time before time, and the light was oh so new to this world and King Lee was a warrior like no other kind.*) Kingu.

KINGU: Yes, my queen.

QUEEN FA'TIMA: Leo will be fine (*smiles*).

KINGU: Thanks, my queen (*smiles*).

QUEEN FA'TIMA: You're welcome. I must be off now, so keep up your training! (*runs off*)

ZIN: I fear there's a darkness coming, Va'li. And we will have to choose a side.

VA'LI: Oh, great one. You've been saying that for so many seasons now.

FAY'FAY: Don't be questioning his wisdom, Va'li!

FAY'FAY

VA'LI: No! I'm just saying, many seasons have came and went, but the vision hasn't come to pass.

ZIN: Leave him be! He doesn't understand as you. Your brother's love is stronger than everything dark (*looks sad thinking about his brothers*).

ZIN

KI: What does that mean, Father?

ZIN: We all fight with the ones we love, wrong or right, but some love is cold as ice. A heart that doesn't
feel will leave an empty soul (*remembers his brothers and begins to cough*).

KAM: I think it's time for him to lay down. I'm sorry, but you must go now.

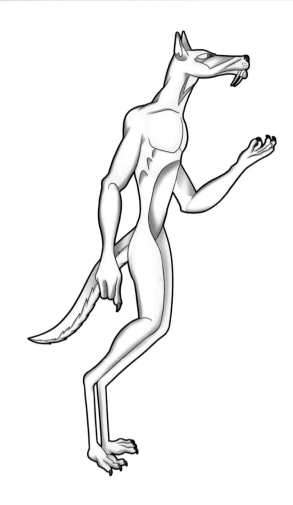

KAM

FAY'FAY: Yes! We understand.

KI: Will he be all right? If a war breaks out at his age…

KAM: The old one will be fine.

VA'LI: I really do think that his vision is making him lose it. (*They leave.*)

FAY'FAY: It's crazy sometimes how he goes off in a daze and says the things he say.

KI: Yep! But everything he said came true (*walks off*).

KI

PRINCE ZWOLLE: Father (*bursts through the palace door*)! Your ways are old and out of season. And you have become weak! Old funji. (*As he walks around the room huffing and puffing!*)

LORD NUNU: My son! You've been lost for many seasons from one to the next! We live in peace for a reason, and war is not the way!

QUEEN GU'DET: Hear your father, my son. You will be *funji* one season. But there are some things that you don't understand. That one season will come where you must know our past.

PRINCE ZWOLLE: No! You both are wrong! (*With a cold look in this eyes, and Ninur'ta walks in*)

NINUR'TA: My lord! The Sha'mush have arrived.

LORD NUNU: This must wait. Prepare the tables for them!

NINUR'TA: Yes, my lord!

PRINCE ZWOLLE: See, your ways are old! (*He turns and makes his way out of the palace.*)

QUEEN GU'DET: My son, my son!

LORD NUNU: Let him go, my love. His season to take my place will come. I will speak with him. Now the guest.

NIN'HARSAG: My lord, do you need me to follow him?

NIN'HARSAG

LORD NU'NU: No. Prepare for the Sha'mush!

MARDUK: Prince Zwolle! Prince Zwolle! What's wrong with him? (*Runs with kill in his eyes!*)

PRINCE ZWOLLE: I will show them! I will show them all! (*He runs to the secret path.*) I will become *funji* sooner than he thinks!

He jumps into the trees limb from limb. He stops at the end of the path because he gets this feeling that something is following him. So he turns to see what's behind him, but he can't see anything but the darkness of trees and falling leaves. So he turns back around and jumps down into the Rockie Canyon below. While back up at the end of the forbidden path stands En'lils, looking down at Prince Zwolle making his way down the Rockie Canyon. My prince, my prince, and fades back into the darkness of the forest!

NINUR'TA: Lord Nunu! The Sha'mush.

THE SHA'MUSH: Lord Nunu, another season (*smiles and hugs, giving gifts!*) Now for the reading of the books.

LORD NUNU: Yes! I know.

THE SHA'MUSH: But before we read the laws of this land, there's a problem!

LORD NUNU: A problem! What kind?

THE SHA'MUSH: The herd was attacked!

LORD NUNU: The herd! By whom?

THE SHA'MUSH: We don't know yet, Lord Nunu, but this attack on the herd is not the first.

UUMBI (THE SHA'MUSH KEEPER)

QUEEN FA'TIMA: Come here, Ki'shar. You look troubled, my child. What's wrong?

PRINCESS KI'SHAR: That scent I picked up on when the herd was attacked. I can remember it. I thought that they were all wiped out! I just don't understand.

QUEEN FA'TIMA: My child, we just have to be ready for whatever comes our way.

PRINCESS KI'SHAR: Do you think that Leo will come back in time?

QUEEN FA'TIMA: All we can do is wait. My son is on a path to find himself. (*They look out over the beautiful vast plains of rocks, mountains, hills, waterfalls, trees, and creatures of all kinds, many of which will never be seen again!*)

LEO: Someone is following me!

NARRATOR: He walks through the dense foggy forest with scarecrow trees.foggy Who knows what kinds of creeping and crawling tree-living monsters are in the forest of Omnom!

LEO: I know you're there, so come out now! I can smell you. Stop hiding!

HA'JIR: You're a long ways from home, cat!

LEO: My name is Leo! And why are you following me?

HA'JIR: This is my land that you're trespassing on!

LEO: I'm just passing through! So let me pass so I can be on my way.

HA'JIR: Let you pass! You didn't say let you pass!

LEO: Yes!

HA'JIR, *begins to laugh*: After I take your head!

Ha'jir now comes from behind a scarecrow tree, drawing his sword and jumping into the air. He kicks, punches, and ducks (as the sparks and sound of their blades forge). But Leo is too skilled in his ways for Ha'jir! With his special move called the shadow claw, he blindsides Ha'jir with a move that he didn't see coming, and down he went with his sword in hand!

LEO, *with the tip of his blade at the throat of Ha'jir*: I'm not your enemy, and besides, it's better to gain a friend than an enemy.

HA'JIR: I understand you now.

LEO: Yes.

HA'JIR: My name is Ha'jir!

LEO: Yes, my name is Leo, and I'm on my way to the Valley of the Kings.

HA'JIR: Why are you going to that place? I've been there.

LEO: So you know where it is?!

HA'JIR: Yes.

LEO: Take me!

HA'JIR: No! It's too dangerous. Some have gone, but never came back!

LEO: I can't turn back now! I have to go there. It's the only way that I can find out who I am.

HA'JIR: I see! I'm the last of my kind, Leo. Yes, I will help you, my friend.

ELEVEN: The light in the heavens are laying itself down. That's enough of training!

O'ANNES: Yes! Because Ni'nib is just too slow now to keep up with us! (*He starts laughing!*)

NI'NIB: I'll show you who's slow! (*Runs behind him*)

ELEVEN: Enough of this!

KINGU: Eleven is right, so knock it off, you two! We must be ready for whatever happens!

O'ANNES: She's still slow.

GAGA: When will he return?

GAGA

ELEVEN: I don't know when he will return. But this power that he's looking for has to be greater than we've ever seen.

O'ANNES: He needs to come back with a snack.

NI'NIB: That's it! (*As she runs off!*)

KINGU: Where are you going?

GAGA: She'll be back. She just needs some time to herself, that's all. And we all know that she's never been hit before in a fight. Just let her deal with it.

BA'LAR: Prince A'nu! Tonight is the second moon.

PRINCE A'NU: I know that, Ba'lar! Everything is going as planned. Soon, my friend, we will have it all.

AN'LB: Yes! Everything.

HA'SAN: Prince A'nu! Prince A'nu! (*He runs through to the lair doors*)

PRINCE A'NU: What is it?

HA'SAN: I've come with news, sir!

HA'SAN

BA'LAR: Tell us now!

HA'SAN: Prince A'nu! Lord Nunu has a brother!

AN'LB: The lies you tell. Kill him!!

HA'SAN, knees shaking, as if they have a mind of their own: No! No! No! It's true.

BA'LAR: Talk!

HA'SAN: As per legend (*As a vision appears*), many seasons ago, long before there was peace between the kingdoms, Lord Nunu and his brother were the best, and nothing could stand in their path. Until one season, they were asked to lead them, but the brothers said no! But this only made them mad, controlled by the darkness that these mad magicians had. One by the name of En'lils! He was very displeased by Nunu's arrogance! He cursed and put a spell on his brother to pay him back for what they had done. But the spell was so powerful Nunu's brother went mad, killing everything around him! They tried to stop him, but no one could. Not even Nunu was a match for him. He just was uncontrollable! En'lils wanted him to lead them, but Nunu said no! "So what have you done, En'lils?" said Nunu. "Your brother will lead us, and this land will be ours!" So Nunu got the best warriors that he could find and went to war with his brother! But Nunu didn't want to kill his brother. So he came up with a plan to save his life and the life of his brother. During the battle, Nunu led his brother to the mountain where the war ended because legend has it that Nunu trapped his brother in the mountains alive. And as for En'lils and his followers, they were banned to the shadows of the forest that surround their kingdom!

EN'LILS

AN'LB: So you want us to believe that Lord Nunu has a brother who lost his mind because of some spell?! By who?

HA'SAN: En'lils.

AN'LB: Hmmm! By En'lils, and he got so powerful until they had to lock him in the mountains?! (*He starts laughing!*) Now I will eat you!

HA'SAN: Prince A'nu! It's true. It's true. I tell you, please!

An'lb: Prince A'nu, let me eat his bones! (*Walks up to him licking his lips, as if to say, "A fresh meal!"*)

HA'SAN: No, Prince A'nu! No! It's true! (*As Val'sae walks in.*)

AN'LB: How do you know?

PRINCE A'NU: An'lb, ease off. So this is true, Val'sae?

VAL'SAE: Yes, it is.

VAL'SAE

PRINCE A'NU: If I go to the mountain, how would I know the right place to look for him?

VAL'SAE, *laughs*: I will tell you how to find him.

BA'LAR: Prince A'nu, do you think that it is wise to free this thing? I mean, sir, they trapped him?

PRINCE A'NU: Yes, Ba'lar, it is better for us because now we can go forward with our plan and take control of this entire land at once. (*He giggles, and they all start to laugh when Kin'sikaah runs in.*)

KIN'SIKAAH: Prince A'nu, Prince A'nu!

PRINCE A'NU: What is it now, Kin'sikaah?! (*breaks his gaggle!*)

KIN'SIKAAH: It's Zwolle, sir. He's here!

PRINCE A'NU: That's very good, Kin'sikaah! He's just in time. But how can you be late for your own death? (*As they all continue laughing again!*)

NARRATOR: In the middle of the night with the stars looking like fireflies sparkling in the heavens, the beasts of the fields get their bellies full off the fruits of the land. But there's another creature that's unlike the rest! He flies the night sky unseen by anything! Many seasons have come and gone as he lands down in front of the mammoth tree that sits in the middle of all the kingdoms!

KWANJU'LI: It's been so long. (*He takes a very, very deep breath and blows a flame of fire that engulfs the whole tree! But it doesn't burn it up. Instead, the tree consumes the flames from the fire like a globe growing and getting bigger!*) I will see you again, my friend. (*He disappears in the blink of an eye, back into the darkness of the night sky, unseen and unheard, just like the many seasons before!*)

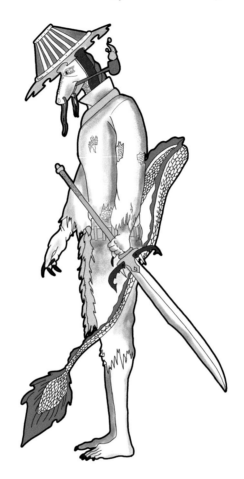

KWANJU'LI

E'NAMA: Lord Nunu, the Sha'mush is right. Why would someone attack the herds like that?

NINUR'TA: The question is not why, but who will do something like this?!

LORD NUNU: Yes, you're right. Who would do a thing like this?

NIN'HARSAG: I will find out who did this, my lord!

E'NAMA: Do you think that the pride had something to do with this?

LORD NUNU: No, E'nama, the pride wouldn't do something like this at all.

MAR'DUK, *takes a drink*: All we can do is wait.

NIN'HARSAG: Wait for what? So we can see if anyone leaves us food this season?!

LORD NUNU: My love, what do you think about this?

QUEEN GU'DET: It's been peace between us and the pride for as long as I can remember. They're not the ones!

LORD NUNU: You're right, my queen.

QUEEN GU'DET: I trust the pride. We all should!

E'NAMA: What if you're wrong about them, my queen?

QUEEN GU'DET: Let us hope that I'm not!

PRINCE A'NU, *with a low growl*: I've been expecting you.

PRINCE ZWOLLE: You know that I hate waiting, A'nu!

PRINCE A'NU: Don't think that you can just come here and boss me around. You better think again, Zwolle!

PRINCE ZWOLLE: You fool! Watch what you say to me, or you will be an ant under my heal, A'nu! (*He walks up to A'nu with his dark-green aura*)

PRINCE A'NU, *with a calm tone, as if to say, "You don't know what's coming"*: You're right, Funji. What would you have me do?

PRINCE ZWOLLE: We must execute our plan at once. I can't wait any longer. It's my time now. My father's ways are over now. He's done! And when I take control of my new kingdom, we must do this when the Sha'mush gives you the laws for this season. That's when we strike! (*He is unaware his life is about to get taken, so Prince A'nu starts gaggling low, gradually getting higher.*) What's funny, A'nu?

PRINCE A'NU: Since you've been trying to find a way to overthrow your father, I put a little plan together myself! (*His facial expression changes with haste, and his gaggling suddenly stops.*)

PRINCE ZWOLLE: What do you mean?

PRINCE A'NU: What do I mean? (*As A'nu menaces, slowly surrounding Zwolle, who is now the prey*) Let's just say with your death, I'll rule all the kingdoms. Attack! (*With a sinister gaggle*)

PRINCE ZWOLLE: I will destroy all of you! (*His eyes turn cold black, and all the hate that he had for his father is now unleashed. He kicks, punches, ducks, jumps, kicks, with the sounds of their blades hitting Zwolle*). That's all you've got! (*Jumps, jumps, kicks, kicks, punches, punches, flips, flips. Ducks, ducks, ducks, flips, flips, flips, punches, kicks, ducks, with the movement of their weapons missing Zwolle, as if he isn't standing there! Flips, flips, sweeps, sweeps, punches, kicks, with a roar!*)

BA'LAR: He's too strong!

PRINCE A'NU: Yes, but keep attacking him! (*He continues giggling and punches, punches, punches, kicks, kicks, swings hatchets.*)

KIN'SIKAAH: Prince A'nu! We have to put an end to this! (*Jumps, jumps, swings, swings, swings*)

PRINCE A'NU: Leave this to me. Everyone, back off. This is my fight from this point!

PRINCE ZWOLLE: You can't defeat me alone, A'nu! You need all the help that you can get! (*With his overconfident, self-arrogant ways and the hatred for his father, it leaves him open to having the worst weakness of all*)! My strength is all I need.

AN'LB: We must fight him together!

PRINCE A'NU: No! He's mine.

PRINCE ZWOLLE: Come on, you fool!

NARRATOR: With their weapons in hand, and so much hatred within them, there will be blood as they run full steam ahead at one another. But Prince A'nu was holding something back, but what was it? As he's watching Prince Zwolle make his move, Prince A'nu sees a vision about his father and his father's last words. And when the vision is over, a sound came from Prince A'nu that none of his minions have ever heard before! He takes one of his hatchets and throws it at him, knowing that Prince Zwolle will move out of its way. But before Prince Zwolle can turn to see where he is, he is gone. Prince Zwolle looks quickly around for him. Then he looks up, and there he is, coming down with his other hatchet in hand with the force that has Prince Zwolle in a daze, stiff and can't move! The blade hit him so quick that he doesn't feel a thing piercing his armor as he falls to the ground dead!

PRINCE A'NU: Now who's the ant?

BA'LAR: Well done, my prince, well done!

KIN'SIKAAH: Now what do we do?

PRINCE A'NU: An'lb!

AN'LB: Sir.

PRINCE A'NU: Where's that piece of cloth?

AN'LB: It's right here, sir.

KIN'SIKAAH: What's that for?

PRINCE A'NU: Just watch and see! (*He wipes the piece of cloth all over the body and places it in his hand.*)

AN'LB: What's that for?

Prince A'nu stands back to his feet.

PRINCE A'NU: There's something else here!

BA'LAR: Yes! I can smell it. (*Everyone sniffs the air after the scent.*)

KIN'SIKAAH: Yes! I can smell it now! Not too many feet away in the swamp, hidden behind an old gray tree!

FON'DU (VO): Oh no! I think that they know that I'm here!

FON'DU

PRINCE A'NU: I know you're out there! Stop hiding and come out now!

FON'DU (VO): I can't come from hiding because if they see me, they will kill me!

PRINCE A'NU: Come out slow! Show yourself, and I will let you live!

FON'DU (VO): What shall I do? I know they are going to ask me if I saw anything. No! I must go now, or they will kill me too! (*He takes off, running for his life.*)

BA'LAR: It's moving!!

PRINCE A'NU, *with a growl*: Don't just stand there. Go after it now!

FON'DU: They're coming, I have to move faster! (*runs for dear life*)

AN'LB: It's over there!

BA'LAR: Don't let it get away!

FON'DU: I can't let them catch me! (*He runs through the swamp.*)

KIN'SIKAAH: We can't let it get away! We have to catch it before it gets on pride land. Now get it!

They run and jump over broken-down tree limbs.

BA'LAR: Stop your talking and just move faster!

NARRATOR: But not too far away, Ni'nib is off to herself replaying the fight she had a few lights ago—"days."

NI'NIB: Maybe I am getting slow (*walks and talks to herself*)! O'annes doesn't know what he's talking about (*laughs, and just then, her thoughts are cut short as her ear picks up a movement*)! Something is coming.

FON'DU: I got to get away. I got to get away! (*Runs with everything in him*)

NI'NIB: What's that scent?

KIN'SIKAAH: Hurry up. We don't have much time to waste! Oh my, we're on pride land now!

NI'NIB: There's more of them coming this way! (*She runs to find out what's going on and sees An'lb!*) That's him!

AN'LB: That's her! (*He stops running.*)

BA'LAR: Her who?

AN'LB: The one I fought with!

KIN'SIKAAH: I don't see anyone, so why'd we stopped running?

AN'LB: Quiet! And just look over there. She sees us! (*looks through the woods right into the eyes of Ni'nib*)

KIN'SIKAAH: I see her. What are we going to do?

Ba'lar: Nothing!

NI'NIB: It's him! I won't let you get away this time! (*With kill in her eyes, she takes off like the wind, weapons in hand, running head-on at her target, An'lb.*)

BA'LAR: We must go now!

KIN'SIKAAH: Why are we running?

AN'LB: There's no time. We must hurry back across now!

NI'NIB: Come back and fight, you cowards! (*runs behind them, yelling*) Come back and fight! I'll get you, if that's the last thing I do. Do you hear me? (*She watches them get away, crossing back over to the wastelands.*)

HA'JIR: Why do you want to go to this place?

LEO: I need to know what's inside of me, and by going to this place, I will find my answer there!

HA'JIR: Well, my friend, you don't have to wait any longer.

LEO: Why?

HA'JIR: Because we're here! (*Now leaving out of the denseness of the fog, looking around to see dry land of sand rocks and hills as far as the eye could see, nothing but sand.*)

LEO: So this is the Valley of the Kings?

HA'JIR: Nope, we have to cross through the two sands! So what are we waiting for?

LEO: Nothing! (*Off they went across the Yhauna sands.*)

HA'JIR: What do you feel, Leo?

LEO: Maybe it's nothing, but stay close and keep your eyes open!

HA'JIR: Right! (*as they're running through the heat and hot dry air of the desert*) We're here now, Leo!

NARRATOR: After running for miles, they finally reach the Valley of the Kings. Still dry land, but never seen before in this light! As they are walking through the Valley of the Kings with their eyes on everything that moves but the ground, the more they move, the ground moves along with them!

HA'JIR, with a low voice: Do you hear something, Leo?

LEO: What is that? (*They stop and key in on their surroundings.*)

HA'JIR: It's nothing!

NARRATOR: But before they can take another step, boom! Jumping from under the sand were catlike creatures armed with weapons surrounding them. And the name of the sand cats are Pa'majsh!

HA'JIR: Watch yourself, Leo.

NARRATOR: They begin fighting with the sand cats, swinging and missing them as they disintegrate back into sand and back to their form again, jumping, kicking, punching, and ducking but still not killing them!

HA'JIR: Leo, how do we destroy these things?

LEO: I don't know yet!

HA'JIR: It's too many of them! (*Kicks, ducks, flips, jumps*) We can't keep this up for long! (*Punches, kicks, kicks, kicks*)

Leo: I know! (*And at that moment, Leo's sword cuts the ear off one of the Pa'majsh, and it turns back into sand*) Cut their ears off!

Ha'jir: Will do! (*And they cut the ears off the Pa'majsh, but except for one*)

Leo: Drop your weapon, and why were you attacking us? Say something! My name is King Leo, and I need to see my father. Please help me! (*But the Pa'majsh just stands there, looking at them.*) I'm going to ask you one more time!

Ha'jir: You're a king?

Leo: Yeah, somewhat. Why?

Ha'jir: You never said that you were a king!

Leo: Yeah, you ain't ask either. (*As he turns back around to the Pa'majsh*)

Ha'jir: Well put. So what are we going to do with this one, kill it like the others?

Leo: Yes, we are! (*walks up to the Pa'majsh*)

Pa'majsh: Wait!

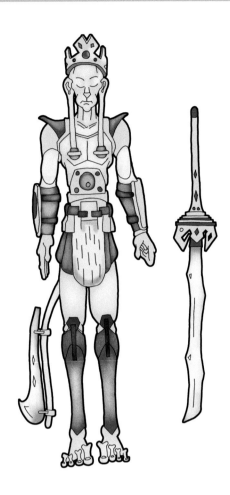

PA'MAJSH

HA'JIR: So you can talk?

PA'MAJSH: Yes, I can.

HA'JIR: Well, good then. Now tell me why you things attacked me and my friend?

PA'MAJSH: We are the protectors of this land, and you're not allowed here on these grounds.

HA'JIR: Okay, protector, whatever you are. Look, my friend is looking for his father. Now either you can help us, or back to the ground with you!

PA'MAJSH: I can't help you.

HA'JIR: So you're no good to us then! (*Puts his sword to its ear*)

PA'MAJSH: No! I said that I can't help you. But I didn't say that I didn't know who could help you!

LEO: Who?

PA'MAJSH: Come and see for yourself! (*They walk with the Pa'majsh through the valley of sand and rocks*) Do you feel that?

LEO: Feel what?

HA'JIR: I can't feel anything!

PA'MAJSH: Time!

LEO: What do you mean, time?

PA'MAJSH: We're here!

HA'JIR: There's nothing here. I see the same sand and rocks. You tricked us!

LEO: Wait, Ha'jir! I can feel something now!

HA'JIR: How can you feel it, but I can't?

LEO: I don't know!

PA'MAJSH: Just watch! (*He closes his eyes and lets out a sound, and the ground quickly starts to shake*)

HA'JIR: What's going on? (*He looks at Leo, but he's just standing there, watching and waiting, not saying a word. And once the shaking stops, the rocks that are on the ground around them start to move. And the movement of the rocks begins to rise up off the ground, forming into the shape of a door.*)

PA'MAJSH: It's done!

HA'JIR: Now what?

PA'MAJSH: Now we go through.

HA'JIR: Through what? (*looks at the rocks from one side to the other*)

LEO: I'll go through!

HA'JIR: No, Leo! You can't. You don't know what this is, my friend.

LEO: I have to find out. There's no turning back now, my friend.

HA'JIR: Okay, if you are going through my friend, he's coming with us!

PA'MAJSH: No, I can't!

HA'JIR: It's a trick, I tell you!

PA'MAJSH: No! I can only open the door, but I can't go through.

HA'JIR: He's lying! (*Leo looks at them both and turns to the door of the rocks and walks through, then vanishes while Ha'Jir runs behind him! As they vanished through the door, the rocks returned to the ground, and the sand cats turned to the sand as the wind blows.*)

PRINCE A'NU: Where is it?

BA'LAR: It got away from us.

AN'LB: A cat showed up, sir! We had to turn around.

PRINCE A'NU: Well, did you at least see what it was?

BA'LAR: No, sir.

KIN'SIKAAH: Now what do we do?

With looks of who and what to blame, Ha'san runs in.

HA'SAN: Prince A'nu, Prince A'nu!

PRINCE A'NU: What is it now?

HA'SAN: The Sha'mush is on their way here, sir.

PRINCE A'NU: Now?

HA'SAN: Now, sir.

PRINCE A'NU: You two, Ba'lar and An'lb, hide his body, and you two come with me now! (*They walk in a rush out of his chamber doors.*)

VAL'SAE: Queen Neffa! (*He announces the welcoming of the Sha'mush, walking in with their books in hand, and the queen gives her welcome.*)

SHA'MUSH: Queen Neffa.

QUEEN NEFFA

QUEEN NEFFA: Sha'mush! Welcome, welcome, the great Sha'mush!

SHA'MUSH: We're here for the reading of the books for this season!

QUEEN NEFFA: Yes. Shall we start?

SHA'MUSH: As you wish. So Prince A'nu is not with us? (*looks around to see if he can see something out of place*)

VAL'SAE: He's right here. (*He and Kin'sikaah along with Ha'san walk in.*)

SHA'MUSH: Well, let's get started! (*Everyone gets to their seats to hear the reading of the law.*) Now before we read, I have some news!

PRINCE A'NU: News of what kind?

SHA'MUSH: The herd was attacked by some unknown creatures. Have any of you heard of such creatures? (*looks around at them as if to say, "I know y'all have something to do with this."*)

PRINCE A'NU: No, Sha'mush. Knowing *that the Sha'mush will destroy anyone and anything that breaks the laws.*) But you will be the first to know! (*breathes hard with that "I'm going to kill An'lb" look on his face*)

SHA'MUSH: No one breaks the laws of this land. But there was one who thought that he could just take what wasn't his! The powers of the Sha'mush keeps order, so there is enough for everyone and everything!

PRINCE A'NU: How dare you! (*slams his hands down on the table as he stands!*)

QUEEN NEFFA: A'nu! Calm yourself. I'm so sorry, great Sha'mush, for this! (*She jumps from her seat around to where A'nu is!*) You must go now and thanks for the law's great Sha'mush. (*The Sha'mush gets up from his seat to leave, but before the Sha'mush leaves from them, he turns to them!*)

SHA'MUSH: Queen Neffa, I want you to remember this! For the one who breaks the laws of this land must be put to death! (*He looks at Prince A'nu, and Prince A'nu looks back at him.*)

NI'NIB: O'annes, O'annes! (*She's running up to him at full speed.*)

O'ANNES: Who are you? (*plays as if he doesn't know who she is and starts laughing*)

NI'NIB: We have no time to play, O'annes. Where is Kingu?

O'ANNES: Right. He's with Eleven.

NI'NIB: Come. We must go find them!

O'ANNES: Why? Hey, what's going on?

NI'NIB: I'll tell you when we find them. Let's go!

KINGU: This season has changed a lot.

ELEVEN: Yes, Kingu, the past seasons are long ago now, so many wars we've fought, many lives lost. But I fear that the greatest war ever is still yet to come! (*As he looks to the heavens*)

KINGU: What war?

NI'NIB: Kingu, Kingu! (*She runs up to them, breaking the train of thought that they are in.*)

KINGU: Yes, what is it, Ni'nib?

NI'NIB: I saw him again!

ELEVEN: Him who?

NI'NIB: That thing that attacked the herds!

KINGU: When did you see him?

NI'NIB: Just now and he was with two more of them. And I think that they were after something, but I don't know what it was. It has its scent.

O'ANNES: Where did they go?

NI'NIB: They got away from me. I chased them, guess where to though—back across there! (points her finger over at Prince A'nu's land).

KINGU: Why would they cross over on our land like that? Something's not right about this.

ELEVEN: The question is not why they crossed, but what they were after is the real question?!

NI'NIB: So what do we do now?

ELEVEN: Ni'nib!

NI'NIB: Yes.

ELEVEN: Now that you have the scent of what they were after, find it and bring it back here before they do. Now go!

NI'NIB: Right! (*turns and off she goes like the wind is carrying her*)

KINGU: What's going on?

ELEVEN: Something is not right about this. Come, let's inform the others.

O'ANNES: Let them know what?

ELEVEN: Even I don't know what's going on, O'annes.

KINGU: Let's get the others!

ELEVEN: We must go! (*They start jogging back to the palace from the outpost.*)

NIN'HARSAG: My lord, I have news, sir.

LORD NUNU: Do tell!

NIN'HARSAG: I found a pride camp, sir.

LORD NUNU: Well, go on!

NIN'HARSAG: Well, sir, they were all dead.

LORD NUNU: Did you see who did it?

NIN'HARSAG: No, sir! Just the dead bodies.

NINUR'TA: Who would do something like this? First the attack on the herd, and now this!

E'NANMA: You're right, Ninur'ta! Something is not right about this.

LORD NUNU: It's been peaceful between us and the pride for many seasons, and now this! (Na'bu just stands there listening.)

QUEEN GU'DET: Maybe it was the That-mus?

LORD NUNU: Maybe! (*He thinks to himself that they won't dare do something like this and that it had to be something else.*)

MAR'DUK: Let us all have a drink! (*takes a swig from one of his bota wine bags*)

E'NANMA: Drink, drink, drink. That's all you do is drink!

MAR'DUK: If you know like I know, then you'd drink too! (*He begins to laugh.*)

NIN'HARSAG: Lord Nunu, what now?

LORD NUNU: Nothing. Everything will show itself! (*looks at his wife*)

NI'NIB (VO): (As she looks around where she first got the scent of the unknown creature, she thinks to herself) I know your scent is still here, but where? (She drops to the ground on one knee and picks up leaves that made some tracks while closing her eyes and taking a deep sniff and at once opens her eyes.) I got you! (Having the full scent of the creature, she stands, and just like that, she is off with the wind, leaving nothing but leaves settling!

BA'LAR: What's taking the prince so long? He should've been back by now.

AN'LB: Yes! But what's he going to do with his body?

PRINCE A'NU: I'll tell you about what I'm going to do!

KIN'SI KAAH: Prince A'nu, do tell.

PRINCE A'NU: I'm going to take Zwolle's body back to his father and tell him that the pride killed him.

BA'LAR: Do you think that's going to work, my prince?

PRINCE A'NU: Yes, his body has the scent of one of the pride on him, so yes. I've seen the whole thing. (*laughs*)

NINUR'TA: Is there something troubling you, my lord?

LORD NUNU: Yes, old friend.

NINUR'TA: Do tell, sire.

LORD NUNU: It's my son. Maybe he's right. Maybe it is time for me to let him become *funji* (ruler/king).

NINUR'TA: Why do you say such things, my lord?

LORD NUNU: My season has come, old friend. (*looks upon the night moon*)

NINUR'TA: We've fought side by side for many seasons now, my lord. And if you think that this is the season for you to be no longer *funji*, then I'll still be here for you, but what about him up there getting freed, my lord?

LORD NUNU: That's what I fear most: the season he escapes and the sadness of so many lives that will be lost.

GUARD: Intruders, intruders, intruders.

LORD NUNU: What's going on!

NINUR'TA: I'll see, my lord.

GUARD: Who are you, and why are you here?

PRINCE A'NU: I'm here to see Lord Nunu.

NIN'HARSAG: Who is it?

GUARD: It's Prince A'nu.

NIN'HARSAG (VO): Prince A'nu—he knows better than to come here.

NIN'HARSAG: What do you want?

PRINCE A'NU: I must speak with Lord Nunu. I have something for him.

NINUR'TA: Who is it, Nin'harsag?

NIN'HARSAG: It's Prince A'nu, and he says that he's got something for our Lord Nunu.

NINUR'TA: What is it that he has?

NIN'HARSAG: He didn't say, so what now?

NINUR'TA: Let them in. It must be something that's brought him here.

NIN'HARSAG: Guards! Let them in.

GUARD: Enter.

NINUR'TA: You know the law of the land by you coming here this way?

PRINCE A'NU: That I do, but I have something, and my lord Nunu will want what I have for him.

NINUR'TA: What is this that you have that has made you break the law, "prince"?

PRINCE A'NU: Show them, Ba'lar.

BA'LAR: Take a look for yourself. (*He opens the top on a large dark box.*)

NINUR'TA: Kill them. (*pulls swords*)

PRINCE A'NU: No! Wait! It wasn't I who've done this.

NINUR'TA: Take them to Lord Nunu *now*!

GUARDS: Move it now!

LORD NUNU: (Lord Nunu sits upon his throne when in walks Queen Gu'det along with their daughter, Princess Ki'shargal, and E'nanma) Is everything all right?

E'NANMA: I don't know, my lord.

QUEEN GU'DET, walks farther in the room: Is there something wrong?

LORD NUNU: I sent Ninur'ta to find out what's going on.

PRINCESS KI'SHARGAL: What's going on?

QUEEN GU'DET: We don't know yet.

NINUR'TA: My lord.

LORD NUNU: What is it, Ninur'ta?

NINUR'TA: You must see this for yourself, my lord (*motions toward the door*). Bring them in.

LORD NUNU: Why are you here? Tell me why I should not kill you for breaking the law of this land.

PRINCE A'NU: Because I have something that belongs to you, Lord Nunu.

LORD NUNU: Well, what is it that you have for me, A'nu?

PRINCE A'NU: Show him, Ba'lar.

BA'LAR: Yes, I will, sire (*once more opens the top of the large dark box*).

NINUR'TA: Wait!

Ba'lar stops and looks at Prince A'nu.

LORD NUNU: Wait for what, Ninur'ta? What's going on here?

NINUR'TA: My lord, it's Prince Zwolle.

LORD NUNU: Zwolle? Where is he, Nin'harsag? Go and tell him I must speak with him at once.

NINUR'TA: No, my Lord, Prince Zwolle is here!

QUEEN GU'DET: What do you mean, Ninur'ta, he's here?

NIN'HARSAG: My queen, you don't have to see this. You shouldn't see this.

LORD NUNU: What do you mean, Nin'harsag? And what's this box for?

PRINCESS KI'SHARGAL: Mother, what's going on?

QUEEN GU'DET: I don't know, my child.

LORD NUNU: I'm going to ask you one more time, Ninur'ta, what's the box for?

NINUR'TA: My lord, I'm sorry to tell you this, but it's Prince Zwolle.

LORD NUNU: Where? (*As Ninur'ta looks in the box*)

QUEEN GU'DET: My son? It can't be!

LORD NUNU: No! You liar!

PRINCESS KI'SHARGAL: No, Mother. (*cries uncontrollably in the arms of her mother after hearing of her brothers' death*)

LORD NUNU: You murdered my son? Now you will die. (*With blood in his eyes, Lord Nunu hits Prince A'nu, dropping him to the floor, then picking him back up over his head and throwing him across the room*). Now die. I say, die!

NINUR'TA: No, my lord! (*As Nin'harsag, E'nanma, and himself tries to hold on to him*)

LORD NUNU: Release me now! Release me I said!

NIN'HARSAG: No, my lord. Calm yourself, please, sire.

NINUR'TA: My lord, let him speak. He has grave news to tell you, sire.

LORD NUNU: You will die. I said release me now.

QUEEN GU'DET: Calm yourself, my love, and let him speak, please.

E'NANMA: Speak now! Tell us what you know at once.

PRINCE A'NU, *gathers himself up off the floor*: It was the pride that did this to your son, not I, sire.

LORD NUNU: Liar! Release me!

QUEEN GU'DET: Prince A'nu, is what you say true?

Na'bu, with his swords at the neck of Ba'lar, slightly cuts him.

E'NANMA: How do we know that you're not lying, Prince A'nu? (*holds back Lord Nunu with everything they have*)

PRINCE A'NU: Just look for yourself. He still has the scent of the pride on him. I saw them kill him.

PRINCESS KI'SHARGAL: Why would they do something so treacherous, Mother?

QUEEN GU'DET: I don't know, my child. I just don't know!

E'NANMA: If what you claim is true, Prince A'nu, why would they do this?

LORD NUNU: Who was it that killed my son, Prince A'nu?

PRINCE A'NU: It was Leo!

Everyone looks at one another.

EVERYONE: Leo?

LORD NUNU: Leo did this to my son?

PRINCE A'NU: Yes, he did. I tried to stop him, but I was too late, Lord Nunu.

QUEEN GU'DET: But why would Leo do this? He knows the laws of the land.

PRINCESS KI'SHARGAL: No, Mother, it can't be, not Leo!

LORD NUNU: Release me so I can see my son, Ninur'ta. (*He breaks down, and they did as told. But knowing for sure that his son can't be dead, Lord Nunu takes slow steps toward the box with anger building up inside of him and with his heart beating fast! He slowly takes the top off the dark large box, and there right before his very eyes was the body of his only beloved son. A tear drops from his eyes.*) My son. (*He closes his eyes, but with great haste, they open! A scent hits his nose, and he drops to his son's body as if he moved! So he starts sniffing his son's body, and with every whiff, he gets madder and more enraged! It is the scent of a cat.*) What's this in his hand? (*He opens it. In it was the piece of cloth that Prince A'nu had, so he took it and put it to his nose.*) No!

NINUR'TA: What is it?

LORD NUNU: I want Leo dead now! I want his entire pride wiped out, and don't stop until every cat is dead and demolished, do you hear me? (*As everyone begins planning war strategy, Lord Nunu turns to Prince A'nu*). So, Prince A'nu, how may I reward you for your help?

PRINCE A'NU: The land that was taken from my father, I want it back, and to fight alongside you.

LORD NUNU: Would that be all?

PRINCE A'NU: Yes, that would be all. (*He looks at Ba'lar as if to say, "I told you."*)

LORD NUNU: It's done (*turns around*). From this moon, the land that was taken from the That-mus is now restored back to Prince A'nu!

NARRATOR: When those words came out, everyone looks at one another, wondering what is really going on. All the while, Prince A'nu stands there with a menacing smile on his face, saying to himself, "Yes! The first part of my plan is working, and now I will get them to kill the pride while I pay a visit to my new friend." Then he laughs to himself!

NARRATOR: Now Leo and Ha'jir enter the spirit world of the unbeknownst, a place where the living is not allowed!

HA'JIR: Leo, what's this place?

LEO: This is the resting place for all the kings that were before me. And one season I'll be here! (*They look around at the spirits of those who died from the past.*)

HA'JIR: So all these cats here were all kings at one season?

LEO: Yes.

HA'JIR: But not right now?

LEO: No! Not now.

And then a voice speaks to him.

MOCGITES: Who are you, and why have you come?

MOCGITES

LEO: Show yourself! My name is King Leo, the descendant of Yaya, the son of King Lee!

HA'JIR: Leo, Do you think it's wise to talk to whatever it is like that?

LEO: Yes!

HA'JIR: Well, Okay then.

MOCGITES: I'm Mocgites, and this is my world! No one comes here alive, so tell me, descendant of Yaya, why have you come?

LEO: I wish to speak with my father, King Lee!

MOCGITES: No one comes here alive!

LEO: I must speak with my father. My pride depends on me, so I must speak with him!

MOCGITES: I will show myself! (*And the spirit of the unknown appears before them!*) I'll let you speak with your father under one condition!

LEO: Fine! What's your condition?

MOCGITES: When you die, your soul will not come here. It will go to the other side, do you understand?

HA'JIR: Wait! Leo, before you do this, what is the other side? That doesn't sound good!

LEO: I must speak with my father, Ha'jir!

HA'JIR: But your soul will be lost forever! Is that what you want?

LEO: Let me speak with my father! (*He looks at Mocgites.*)

MOCGITES: As you wish! (*And the spirit of his father appears in full form before them!*)

HA'JIR: Oh my! He's…he's…

LEO: Yes! He's my father!

King Lee stands before his son, towering above them.

KING LEE

KING LEE: My son, you've grown to be a fine young prince over the seasons.

LEO: Yes, Father.

KING LEE: You have many questions, my son.

LEO: Yes, I do, Father.

KING LEE: Well, ask your questions, my son.

LEO: There's something inside of me Father, something that's fighting to get out. Why can't I understand what it is Father?

KING LEE: My son, you do understand. You and I are one.

LEO: Father! Help me, please. I don't know what's happening.

KING LEE: My son, that of which is inside of you fighting to get out, it's your true form.

LEO: My true form?

KING LEE: Yes, my son, your true form. That, my son, is why we are one and the same. (*gives his son a knowing look*)

LEO: What are you, Father (*clears his throat*), we, I mean. What are we?

KING LEE, *laughs gallantly*: A liger, the most powerful cat to ever roam the earth.

LEO: Father! Show me how to become a true liger as you are, Father.

KING LEE: Yes, my son. Close your eyes and take everything you love and use it, my son. But remember, never use it for yourself but for your pride that needs you. You can do it, my son. I believe in you. Now believe in yourself. (*With his eyes closed, Leo starts to see visions of his mother and his friend and his son along with the whole pride, the pride that he had to protect along with the faces of everyone in the pride. At once, the vision changes. He can see his dead friends, with his mother and son, also killed. Everyone that he had ever known were now dead.*) Use your anger, my son. Feed off of it.

NARRATOR: And just like that, it happens. He begins to change, his body starts to grow, his arms gets bigger, along with his legs. His teeth even grows longer, but nothing like his father's, who was born a liger. Leo doesn't get the tiger stripes like his father, but he gets everything else, with the horn that grows out the middle of his forehead! But by Leo being born lion and has to transform into a liger, that makes him the most powerful cat that would ever live, and when his vision is over, he lets out a roar that will never be heard again! (*roars!*)

KING LEO: This is your true form, my son!

HA'JIR: Leo, that's you? (*He steps back.*)

LEO: Yes!

HA'JIR: You look…you look!

LEO: I know. Calm down!

KING LEE: You must go, my son. Your pride is waiting for your return. Take this with you, my son. A true king is not a king of war but love and peace!

LEO: Yes, Father. I'll keep it for all seasons to come!

KING LEE: My son! (*He begins to fade away!*)

HA'JIR: We can go now, right, Leo?

LEO: Yes, my friend! (*He looks at his father one last time before he was gone.*)

MOCGITES: No!

LEO: Why? (*He turns at Mocgites in his full form.*)

MOCGITES: Your heart is good, Leo, and the heart of your friend. And I know that he's the last of his kind.

LEO: Yes, he is.

MOCGITES: You know, Leo, that your soul will not rest here! But to the other side it will go. But to your friend as the last of your kind, this will help you throughout the journey!

HA'JIR: What's he talking about, Leo?

LEO: I don't know, Ha'jir! (*He looks at him, then back at Mocgites.*)

MOCGITES: Change now!

HA'JIR: Leo!

LEO: What are you doing to him?

MOCGITES: I'm giving him something that he's going to need, Leo! (*And the change comes as Ha'jir's ears get longer. And his hair goes from a brown to an ice black, and his feet change as well.*) Now take to the heavens! (*Wings grow from his back, with razor-like ends to them as he changes to his new form!*)

LEO: Yes, Ha'jir! Yes.

MOCGITES: Leo, his name is no longer Ha'jir. It's Naf'mu!

LEO: I understand now! (*He looks at his friend in his new form.*)

MOCGITES: You must go now and never return! (*Everything goes white, and Leo along with Naf'mu are standing back in the Valley of the Kings at the entranceway.*)

NAF'MU: Leo, you're not in your liger form anymore?

LEO: No, but I can control it now, my friend! (*He smiles at him.*)

NAF'MU: What now, Leo?

LEO: We go home now! You're a part of my pride now, and we have so many seasons ahead of us!

NARRATOR: As the wind blows with a little dust and with smiles on their faces, Naf'mu spreads his wings, with his sword in hand, woosh. Just like that, into the sky he goes. As Leo looks at him with a smile, he then looks ahead and takes off toward his home with his new power. Now Leo has eyes in the sky, while he himself runs the earth!

NINUR'TA: Lord Nunu, do you think that Leo killed your son?

LORD NUNU: Yes! The scent of one of them was on him.

E'NANMA: I'll tell you what! After we put Prince Zwolle to rest, We go to war with them!

Everyone agrees!

NIN'HARSAG: Yes, we will go to war with them, and everything's awaiting your order, sir!

QUEEN GU'DET: They killed my son, my only son. (*She lies in Nunu's arms.*)

LORD NUNU: They will all pay for this, my love! (*He lets go and turns to Na'bu.*) Na'bu, don't leave a cat standing. An'shar, Ish'kur, follow Na'bu if he needs you, but I know he doesn't! (*Na'bu smiles at him.*) E'nanma, go tell Lah'mu to get the weapons ready.

E'NANMA: Yes, sir!

LORD NUNU: Ninur'ta!

NINUR'TA: Yes.

LORD NUNU: We must put my son to rest before we go to war. Is that clear?

NINUR'TA: Yes, my lord. I know the place to take him. Mar'duk, come with me! (*They turn to leave for the place to put Prince Zwolle to rest.*)

LORD NUNU: In two lights, we will go to war! Come, my love! (*Lord Nunu takes his wife to go see their son's body before the two lights. As he holds her hand and looks in her eyes, he can see the last of their son, Prince Zwolle!*)

FA'HISH: Princess, Princess, where are you running off to? (*runs behind her*)

PRINCESS KI'SHARGAL: I can't stay here! (*She runs to the forest, through the secret path.*)

FA'HISH: Where are you going? Don't leave me. I'm coming too, so wait! (*She stops to wait for her best friend.*) Where are you going, Ki'shargal?

PRINCESS KI'SHARGAL: I'm going to see An'kij!

FA'HISH: Well, I'm going too, and I'm not taking no for an answer, plus Un'ni! (*He jumps out from behind one of the trees.*) So.

PRINCESS KI'SHARGAL: Let's go! (*She hugs her, and all three jump into the trees of the forest.*)

NARRATOR: Now Un'slaw and An'kij are back at his place, somewhere deep in the forest, sitting down, talking, getting to know each other better as friends!

AN'KIJ: Wait! Un'slaw, do you hear that? It sounds like voices!

Un'slaw: Yes! I hear many voices! (*He bellows out a laugh.*)

An'kij: No! I'm not talking about things like that.

Un'slaw: What do you mean?

An'kij: I sometimes hear a voice in my head, plus I see this face. You might think I'm crazy! (*As an uneasy semi crooked smile creeps upon his face*)

Un'slaw: What does this voice say to you?

An'kij: That's the crazy part about it. I can hear the voice, but I can't understand the language that he speaks to me in. And just like tonight right before our fight and, again, just moments ago! (*Not knowing that the voice that he hears and the face that he sees is his father's. So his mother overhears him talking to Un'slaw about the voices and what he's been seeing. Then she walks in on them.*)

Tia'mat: What does this face look like, my son?

An'kij: Mother, I'm sorry. I didn't know that you were here!

Tia'mat: What does this face look like, An'kij? (*gives him that stern look while walking up to him*)

An'kij: Well, Mother, I really can't tell you how he looks because everytime I start to see his face, flames appear like hair from around his face or something!

Tia'mat: Oh no! (*falls to her knees in despair*)

An'kij: What's the matter, Mother? (*rushes up out his seat over to her*)

Princess Ki'shargal: An'kij!

He hears a voice. It's Princess Ki'shargal, leaving his mother without a word and running to the princess, completely forgetting about his mother.

Princess Ki'shargal: It's my brother. He's been killed! The pride killed him. (*hugs him*)

Tia'mat: The pride did what? (*gets up off her knees*) What did you just say?

Fa'hish: The pride killed her brother. You heard her! (she snaps)

Tia'mat: Are you sure that it was the pride??

Princess Ki'shargal: Yes, their scent was all over his body!

An'kij: I'm here now. It's okay.

Tia'mat: No! This is not right, Ki'shargal. You must leave now.

Princess Ki'shargal: No! I will leave your home, but I will not go back there!

Tia'mat: Look, Ki'shargal! You must leave now. Please go!

Princess Ki'shargal, *with a surprised look on her face*: How do you know my name?

And An'kij looks at her as if to say, "She's right because I haven't told you anything about her.

Tia'mat: I can't tell you right now! So please leave, Ki'shargal. A war is coming.

Narrator: Now as Ni'nib is running to find out what it is that they were after, thinking to herself where she is to go off to as she finds herself on the outer lands where all those that go there can't make it in the big kingdom! As she walks through the streets of this peaceful village, she sees all kinds of hurt creatures! Some were missing arms, others missing legs among other things. She walks up to one of the creatures!

Ni'nib: Hi, you there, I'm trying to find someone.

Ku'lus: Who are you looking for?

KU'LUS

Ni'nib: I don't know how he looks, but I've got his scent!

Ku'lus: I can't help you. But I may know who can. Come with me now, please! (*He takes her through the pathways of the village. Down one hill here and up another hill there! A left right here, a right, left, then finally, getting to one that doesn't look much different from the others as they walk in!*) Sir I have someone, and she needs your help.

A'kintoya: Who is it?

Ku'lus: Who are you? (*turns and asks her name*)

Ni'nib: My name is Ni'nib! And my father is of King Lee's pride.

A'kintoya: Welcome, Ni'nib, of the pride come. How can I help?

A'KINTOYA

Ni'nib: I was following a scent, and it led me here. What is this place called?

Baba'la: Why do you look for this creature?

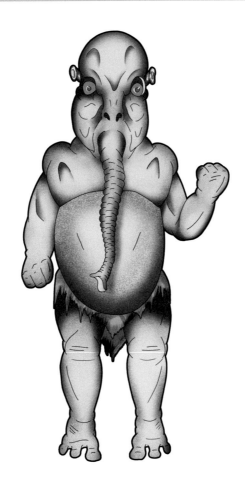

BABA'LA

Ni'nib: It saw something, and I must know what it saw!

A'kintoya: This place where you are is called Ash! It was I who found this place, a place of peace where all are welcome. For my home, I will fight! We will fight, but you come in peace, and I will help you, Ni'nib of the pride. Ku'lus, send for Na'sebu. He's our foreseer of all things.

Ku'lus: Sir!

A'kintoya: Our Na'sebu will find whomever you are looking for.

Ni'nib: I hope you're right!

A'kintoya: What troubles you, my child? Is there something wrong? You don't have to say it. Just know this: we are the ones we fear the most! (*folds her arms*)

Ku'lus: Here he is, sir!

A'KINTOYA: Yes, Na'sebu, my friend, welcome! Welcome! I need your help with something, old friend. Well, she needs help with something.

NA'SEBU: Yes, how can I be of a service to you, ma'am?

NI'NIB: Well, I'm looking for a creature that came here, but I don't know how it looks. All I have is its scent. For the love of the pride! I wish that there was a way, if I only had something!

NA'SEBU: Very well then, I will find whomever that you are searching for! You just have to close your eyes and go back to where you were! Free your mind and see yourself standing there! Listen to the sounds that surround you! Can you smell the air? Feel the wind! Seeing her yourself, standing back on pride grounds. I see your vision. Yes, I can see him! He's running, and there're others behind him. Wait! I can see through his eye's (*meaning An'lb*)! I see you now (*removes his hands from her head*). He's not far from here. We must go now.

NI'NIB: What did you do to me?

NA'SEBU: We must go now!

NI'NIB: Where is he?

NA'SEBU: He's not far from here! He's hiding, but I can take you to him.

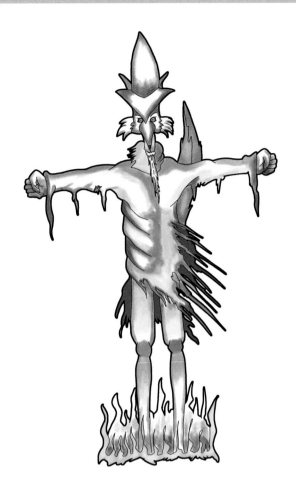

NA'SEBU

NI'NIB: Take me now, and thanks A'kintoya for everything! We pride have only our word. That's the pride way, and you are welcome to my home, sir.

A'KINTOYA: Yes, Ni'nib of the pride, save your home! Let's get on our way to find where this unknown creature is hiding.

NARRATOR: And in no time, they are there, closed off from the others on the end of the village. In a small tent there, he is inside!

NA'SEBU: He's in there.

NI'NIB: So he's in there, you say?

NA'SEBU: Yes! (*walks into the door of the dark tent*) I know that you're here, and I have your scent. You don't have to be afraid of me. It's Okay. You can come out, I just want to ask you some questions, please! Don't be afraid. Come! (*looks around to see if he would come out on his own*) Please I need your help. Why were the That-mus clan chasing you? I've come a long ways for your help!

FON'DU: So you didn't come to kill me?

NASE'BU: No! I just want to know why they were after you.

FON'DU: Okay I'm coming out, so stay where you are and don't move! (*steps out from behind a pillar*) I was out looking for treehoppers. Do you know how sweet they are? But I couldn't find not one hopper, so I kept on looking until I heard something. I didn't know what it was, so I went to see where it was coming from, and then I saw them!

NI'NIB: Them who? Who did you see?

FON'DU: I don't know who they were, but one of them was an ape!

NI'NIB: An ape?

FON'DU: Yes, they were talking about something, but I couldn't hear what they were talking about because whatever it was made them attack him!

NI'NIB: Attacked him, who attacked him?

FON'DU: The ape! He was attacked by the others who were there with him! He fought two of them, but they weren't any match for him. And that's when the leader started fighting himself. The ape was winning until their leader went into a mad rage of power and killed him. I saw the whole thing until it was over, and that's when they heard me. And that's when they started chasing me, but for some reason, they stopped and turned around! So I just kept on running until I didn't see anyone behind me! (*cries*)

NI'NIB: They stopped because they saw me.

FON'DU: Thanks for saving my life.

NI'NIB: Well, you're welcome! But we have no time, Fon'du. You must come with me. Because if what you're saying is true, a war is coming, and you're the only one who can stop it!

FON'DU: Yes, I understand!

NI'NIB: Good, and tell A'kintoya thanks for his help again, Na'sebu!

NA'SEBU, *with a smile*: Yes, I will, Ni'nib of the pride!

NI'NIB: Let's go, Fon'du. Get on my back. We don't have much time! (*With him on her back, she runs at her top speed, leaving out of the village.*)

NIN'HARSAG: My lord, Everything is in place whenever you're ready, sir.

LORD NUNU: Yes! Where is Na'bu and the twins? They should've gotten word to my army by now.

E'NANMA: Here they come now! (*walks in with the twins*)

Na'bu does ancient monkey talk.

LORD NUNU: That's good, Na'bu. We go to war now! And you tell everyone to leave that cat Leo to me! He must pay for what he has done!

EVERYONE: Bambaa-Tu, Bambaa-Tu.

QUEEN GU'DET: My love, my love, Ki'shargal, she's missing!

LORD NUNU: What?

QUEEN GU'DET: She's nowhere to be found. I've looked everywhere. Oh no! What if something has happened to her? (*She cries in his arms*)

LORD NUNU: I will find her! (*lets her go from his arms*). I love you (*kisses her*). We go to war! (*roars*)

NARRATOR: Meanwhile, back with the pride, things are about to take a turn!

ELEVEN: The heavens are about to cry, my queen!

QUEEN FA'TIMA: Yes, it is, Eleven. But more than the cries from the heavens are coming!

LA'PIR, *rushes up to her and gets on one knee*: My queen, my queen.

QUEEN FA'TIMA: Yes, what is it, La'pir?

LA'PIR: We've been attacked by an ape on the land, ma'am. He killed the rest of them. I alone survived!

LA'PIR

QUEEN FA'TIMA: Are you sure that he was an ape?

LA'PIR: Yes, my queen. I'm sure that it was an ape, ma'am. I got away while he was attacking the others!

KINGU: What's wrong?

ELEVEN: We were attacked!

GAGA: By who? Who attacked us!?

QUEEN FA'TIMA: It was an ape!

PRINCESS KI'SHAR: An ape! But why would they attack us? What's going on?

ELEVEN: We don't know yet!

E'NURN: There's a war going on, and we don't know anything about it!

E'NURN

DAU'RU: If there's a war going on, we would know about it!

A'DAPA: Whatever it is that's going on, all I know is that something is not right about this!

PRINCE NANNAR: Mother! So what do we do now?

PRINCESS KI'SHAR: I don't know, my son, but whoever's out there, we'll be ready for them!

O'ANNES: Well, let the games begin!

NIBI'RU: It's Nin'harsag (*runs in*). It's Nin'harsag. She's here!

QUEEN FA'TIMA: What's she doing here?

Now everyone rushes out to find out what's going on! Getting to the front of the pride land, standing in the clearing is Nin'harsag!

PRINCESS KI'SHAR (VO): What does Nin'harsag want? She doesn't like me, and I don't like her, so why would she come here?

NIN'HARSAG: Ki'shar! I see that you still have feelings for me. Well, that same hate I have for you will end this season!

PRINCESS KI'SHAR: What are you talking about? Do any of you know what she's talking about?

NIN'HARSAG: This season is the beginning of many seasons to come! I bring word from Lord Nunu. On the rising of the next light, the Bambaa-Tu will be at war with the pride for the death of Lord Nunu's son, Prince Zwolle! So you cats have until the light to prepare yourselves! (*She flies off laughing.*)

DAU'RU: We've been at peace with the Bambaa-Tu clan for many seasons, and now Lord Nunu wants war for the death of his son (*shakes his head*). Something is not right!

DAU'RU

ELEVEN: I know, my friend, so many seasons ago!

KINGU: But who would do something like this?

PRINCESS KI'SHAR: But for what reason would they kill Zwolle?

A'DAPA: Whoever did this knew what they were doing! Breaking the law is one thing, but killing a prince is another!

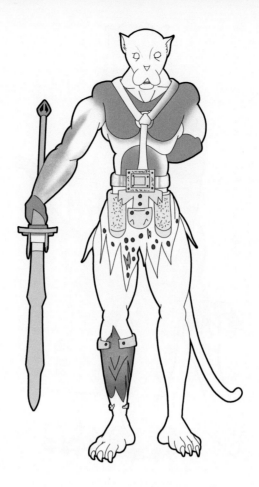

A'DAPA

GAGA: What about Ni'nib, where is she?

ELEVEN: I don't know, and I don't think that she'll be back in time!

E'NURN: Well, if it's war they want, then it's war they get!

O'ANNES: I'm ready for a good fight!

ELEVEN: My queen, what is it that you would like for us to do?

QUEEN FA'TIMA: I don't know!

KINGU: My queen, every one of us here knows the law, and not one of us here killed their prince. But we have to stay strong until Leo and Ni'nib get back here! So if we have to fight, then we fight. Let's just hope that we can hold them off until they return, my queen!

QUEEN FA'TIMA: You're right, Kingu! Someone is behind this. All we have is our word. The heart and soul of a true king lives on! We will fight, and let's just hope that Leo and Ni'nib make it in time!

E'NURN: So we fight?

QUEEN FA'TIMA: Yes! So make sure the army is ready for war. We fight until the return of my son! (*She thinks to herself that it was Leo's father that had made peace with the Bambaa-Tu so many seasons ago!*) Where are you, Leo, my son? We need you. (*looks up at the heavens*)

VAL'SAE: Everything is going to plan, Prince A'nu?

PRINCE A'NU: Yes, it is! And when I find whoever he is that's in the mountain and get him on my side, then the That-mus clan will take over this whole land!

BA'LAR: But do you think that you can control him? My prince, if he's as powerful as they say he is, do you think that you'll be able to, sir?

PRINCE A'NU: We want the same thing. So yes, Ba'lar, he can and will be controlled by me!

VAL'SAE: You must go to the mountain and find out where he is before it's too late, A'nu!

QUEEN NEFFA: My son! (*walks in*) I know that I've been hard on you, but you must understand. I miss your father, and I know that you've been planning something! So do what you will, and get back what's owed to us, my son!

PRINCE A'NU: Yes, Mother! I will do it for Father!

AN'LB: So what do we do now, Prince?

PRINCE A'NU: Ba'lar, Ha'san, An'lb, you are coming with me to the mountain. Oh! Kin'sikaah, you're coming too. I will need you. Ha'san will show us the way through the mountains where our friend is. The rest of you, stay here, and where's Ma'habi?

MA'HABI: Here I am, my prince!

PRINCE A'NU: Good. I need you to come too so you can feel the mountains for our friend!

MA'HABI: Yes, my prince, will do!

PRINCE A'NU, *chuckles gallantly*: This land will be mine!

FON'DU: How are you able to see in the dark like this?

NI'NIB: I'm a cat!

FON'DU: Oh, right! What was I thinking? Are the rest fast like you?

NI'NIB: No! (*She runs through the darkness over hills and around trees at top speed, all while thinking to herself that she has to make it back in time before something very bad happens.*) Leo! Where are you?

NARRATOR: Leo, with his new powers, is like the wind blowing through the air. Along with Naf'mu keeping up from the sky, Leo is thinking to himself, *I have a bad feeling*, as he runs faster and faster!

JIN'DU: Father!

JIN'DU

HA'KIM: Yes, is there something wrong?

JIN'DU: Yes, there is!

HA'KIM: Do tell, my son.

JIN'DU: There will be a war at first light!

HA'KIM: A war with whom?

JIN'DU: A war between the pride and the Bambaa-Tu clan, sir. It's said that Leo killed Prince Zwolle!

HA'KIM: Prince Zwolle is dead, and Leo is the one who killed him? It can't be!

JIN'DU: Yes, Father. It's been said that it was Leo! Father, what's wrong?

HA'KIM: My son, it was King Lee that brought peace between the clans many seasons ago!

JIN'DU: What, are you saying Father—

HA'KIM: A blind monkey can see a lot of things. This wasn't the work of the pride, my son! You two go as well because your brother will need you.

NI'JIM: What about you, Father?

HA'KIM: I will wait here. So go now, my sons!

NARRATOR: As his two sons jumps into the trees, leaving to aid their brother, Ha'kim knows all too well that it wasn't the pride that killed Zwolle. Yes, deep down, he knows that it's a bigger war coming, and not the war at first light!

NARRATOR: With the breaking of light at hand, the whole land is quiet! Not a sound to be heard, as if the land itself is dead! It is the type of quietness right before a great battle, when everyone knows what to do when that time comes. Yes, Lord Nunu knows this feeling all too well. With the loss of his only son, he sits in his chamber all alone with hate in his eyes and one thing running through his mind: "Leo, Leo, Leo, Leo, Leo!" With a scream, the light begins to rise along with Queen Gu'det looking out of her window at the land that will be filled with blood in a short time. But who can sleep with the loss of a child and the other one missing. So she just stands there looking out of the window, thinking about the loss of her children.

LORD NUNU: *War!*

KINGU: It's time! (*looks over the quiet kingdom*)

ELEVEN: Are you ready for this, Kingu?

KINGU: Yes!

ELEVEN: Well done!

NARRATOR: As the light breaks its way through, Kingu makes a sound that can be heard over the whole kingdom—the sound of war!

DAU'RU: To the field!

NARRATOR: She cries out loud, with the pride members out front—Kingu, Gaga, O'annes, Princess Ki'shar, along with Nannar, E'nurn, and A'dapa—but Eleven and Dau'ru stayed back with Queen Fa'tima!

KINGU: To the field! (*stops and calls out to Dau'ru, with the army standing behind her, and looks over the battlefield*)

GAGA: Where are they?

O'ANNES: Maybe they're not coming. (*He laughs ferociously! But before anyone could say another word, across the field was a monkey. And not just any monkey—oh no, it was Na'bu! And O'annes starts to laugh out loud.*) One monkey, is that all?

PRINCE A'NU: Are you sure that this is the way Ha'San?

HA'SAN: Yes, my prince. This is the way, I'm sure of it.

AN'LB: How long do we have before we get to the mountains?

BA'LAR: Yes, we've been walking sometime now, and we haven't arrived there yet!

KIN'SI KAAH: I think that he's lying, Prince!

HA'SAN: No, no, no. It's not that far, my prince, you'll see!

MA'HABI: He's right, my prince. I can feel something as we get closer.

MA'HABI

PRINCE A'NU: Stop! What do you feel, Ma'habi?

MA'HABI: I feel a great power, my prince, and it's coming from ahead.

PRINCE A'NU: Are you sure, Ma'habi?

MA'HABI: Yes, this way! (*They walk through the dark trails, deep up in the mountains.*)

LORD NUNU, *screaming across the field of thick brushes of grass*: Where's Leo?

KINGU, *yelling back across the fields at Lord Nunu*: We can talk about this, and no one has to die, Lord Nunu.

LORD NUNU: Tell me where that backstabbing cat, Leo is, or all of you will die!

KINGU: Do what you must, Lord Nunu. We are the pride of this land—Leo's pride! (*When Kingu said these words, you could hear the beating of their shields and the pounding of their weapons for miles. No one really knows why the heart and soul of a true leader can live on through his pride.*)

NINUR'TA: He gave me a little fire, for he's a good talker.

LORD NUNU: Yes, he is, and he will be the first to die! Attack!

NARRATOR: Both armies race to each other with their weapons in hand, both with one thing on their minds. This is the biggest war of all seasons, and only the strong will survive. The two armies crash at each other as a massive wave hits the base of rocks at the bottom of a cliff, then down comes the rain from the sky.

LORD NUNU, *locked in battle with Kingu*: You all will die for what you've done. (*Kick, punch, punch, kick, duck, flip, flip, punch, kick.*)

NIN'HARSAG: I've been waiting for this many seasons, Princess!

PRINCESS KI'SHAR: Well, the wait is over, Nin'harsag (*The two go at it—swing, punch, punch, kick, swing. Nin'harsag flies up into the air and comes down on Ki'shar.*)

NIN'HARSAG: This day will be your death (*landing on top of Ki'shar*).

GAGA: It looks like you're having fun over there O'annes.

O'ANNES: Why, yes, Gaga! Two monkeys at a time (*laughs*).

GAGA: Okay, with you having so much fun, you need to go and slow that little red one down because he's picking them apart over there, O'annes. (*The little red monkey he speaks of is none other than Na'bu.*)

PRINCESS KI'SHARGAL: We're too late, the battle has already started.

UNSLAW: No, we're just in time.

AN'KIJ: Right, Unslaw! You help them over there, and Ki'shargal, your mother! (*She cuts him off.*)

TIA'MAT: I'll be fine, son, just remember who trained you.

PRINCESS KI'SHARGAL: I have to find my father, An'kij!

AN'KIJ: We are ready. Attack! (*They rush to the battlefield.*)

LORD NUNU: I will kill all of you for what Leo did to my son! (*Their blades meet with each other.*)

KINGU: Leo didn't kill your son! (*He flips out of the way of Lord Nunu's flesh attack.*)

LORD NUNU: You lie (*cutting the heads off two cats that got in the way of him and Kingu fighting*).

O'ANNES: Look at you, little monkey, you are moving too fast. I guess that I have to slow you down. (*Talking to Na'bu, but he just stands there and smiles at O'annes because O'annes doesn't know what he is getting himself into. And out of nowhere, Jin'du and Ni'Jim come jumping out from the tall trees beside him.*) Two more.

NA'BU: Ancient monkey talk?

JIN'DU: Father told us to come.

NA'BU: Ancient monkey talk!

JIN'DU: No, Na'bu! We didn't come to help you. We came to fight!

O'ANNES: Okay! Enough talking. You said that you came to fight, so let's fight.

NA'BU: Ancient monkey talk!

O'ANNES: What are you waiting for!

JIN'DU: He got this! (*As they went off to fight with each other.*)

O'ANNES: No! Don't run off! Hey! Come back! It's going to take more than this little monkey to beat me! (But Na'bu isn't your ordinary monkey, *O'annes thinks*).

Na'bu just smiles at him.

MA'HABI: This is it! (*As they reach the base of the mountain.*)

HASAN: See, see! I told you sir, that I was telling the truth. Do you believe me now, my prince?

PRINCE A'NU: Yes!

BA'LAR: So how do we find out where he's at? (*As each one of them looks far away through the mountain.*)

MA'HABI: I found the way.

PRINCE A'NU: Yes, I see it too.

NARRATOR: As they walk through the hidden trail that has been long forgotten many, many seasons ago, the dark floors of the mountain tells it story with marks of old claws carved on the walls of the mountain and the bones of unknown creatures that turned into stones from the long seasons that came and passed, alongside their weapons. With the sounds of unknown creatures all around them, they keep on walking through the dark trail of the mountain.

AN'LB: We're lost?

NARRATOR: Now after walking some time now, the light in the trail begins to get brighter and brighter. And before anyone could notice, they were coming out the dark trail overlooking the entire kingdom from its highest peak.

BA'LAR: How long has this been here?

MA'HABI: Before your season!

KIN'SI KAAH, *a look of astonishment and amazement on his face*: You can see everything from here.

PRINCE A'NU: We didn't come here for this! Well, where is he?

UNKNOWN VOICE: Go, you don't belong here.

PRINCE A'NU: Who are you? Show yourself!

UNKNOWN VOICE: You don't belong here.

NIN'HARSAG: This light, your pride, will fall, Princess!

PRINCESS KI'SHAR: Never! (*Swing, duck, swing, punch, kick, kick, flip, flip, swing—as their swords ferociously meet.*)

E'NURN: Come on! (*Swing, swing, swing, swing.*)

LORD NUNU, *yelling furiously*: Fight me and stop this running!

KINGU: You can do better than that, can't you? (*Flip, flip, duck, kick, swing, swing, jump kick, kick, block.*)

O'ANNES: So you do have skills, you little red monkey? (*Swings at Na'bu, but Na'bu ducks his blows, jumping over his head, kicking O'annes in the back, making him fall face-down to the ground. O'annes turns his head while on the ground, looking back at Na'bu as he gets up. Na'bu, still with the same look in eyes, hate in his face, shows a grimacing, evil smile.*) You will pay for that. I don't see anything funny. (*Charges full speed at Na'bu.*)

AN'KIJ: Stay behind me, Ki'shargal and Fa'hish (*fights their way throughout the crowd*).

NA'BU: Ancient monkey talk!

O'annes: Come on! (*As he gives it all that he has, but Na'bu is just too skilled for him because every time he swings and kicks, Na'bu would just block the kicks and duck the swing and hit him every time.*)

MA'HABI: You must be Ninsish'zidda?

UNKNOWN VOICE: No! I'm not he!

KIN'SI KAAH: Well, who are you, if not he?

PRINCE A'NU: So who are you?

FI'KUN, *appearing before them from the shadows*: My name is Fi'kun. I'm the guardian of this mountain. So I tell you now, leave or you all will die! (*His voice grows louder with each word.*)

FI'KUN

PRINCE A'NU: No, I can't do that. We've come too far to turn back now. But I'll tell you something: step aside. My fight isn't with you, but if I have to go through you to get to him, then so be it (*getting angry*).

FI'KUN: So you won't leave? Then die! (*Roaring, flying off the top of the mountain.*)

PRINCE A'NU: Attack! (*They begin fighting against Fi'kun. Ba'lar, An'lb, and Kin'si Kaah fight furiously as Prince A'nu watches on. Prince A'nu observes how Fi'kun would swing his tail right before he flies up and comes back down with another attack. So he waits for him to do it again, and just as he did this last time, right before he swings his tail, Prince A'nu jumps off the rocks and catches him in midair. Fi'kun falls to the ground with his arm and wing missing—Booooom—as he crashes to the ground with a hard thud.*)

QUEEN FATIMA: Eleven, can you see them?

ELEVEN: Yes, my queen.

QUEEN FATIMA: How are they holding up?

DAU'RU: The young ones are doing fine, my queen.

ELEVEN: But it looks like O'annes is having some problems with the one he's fighting... Oh no!

QUEEN FATIMA: What's wrong, Eleven?

ELEVEN: Kingu just took a bad hit.

QUEEN FATIMA: How long do you think they can hold up?

ELEVEN: I don't know, my queen. We're falling and we're falling fast.

QUEEN FATIMA: My son, where are you? (*She thinks to herself, just as the rain begins to fall from the heavens, more notably, the first rain of this season.*)

ELEVEN: The heavens are crying, my queen.

QUEEN FATIMA: Yes, I know!

DAU'RU: What's that?

ELEVEN: Where?

DAU'RU: Can't you feel it?

QUEEN FATIMA: What are you talking about, Dau'ru?

DAU'RU: Something or someone is coming, and it's moving fast!

ELEVEN: Where? I don't see anything!

QUEEN FATIMA: Yes, yes, I do feel it now. (*Before they could say another word, there he is. Leo, with the sun beginning to set and the cries from the heavens falling in slow motion, making it look as if a drop of rain isn't landing on him.*) My son! (*A look of pure happiness graces her face, looking at her son from afar.*)

ELEVEN: It's Leo.

DAU'RU: Yes, it is! I told you it was him.

LEO: Am I too late?

ELEVEN: No!

DAU'RU: Welcome back, Leo.

LEO: Thanks!

QUEEN FATIMA: Hurry, my son, because your pride needs you.

LEO: Right mother! (*He passes by his kingdom in his second form, moving at a speed that was new for his mother and the others who are watching him pass by.*)

Queen Fatima: Now we have a *chance*!

O'ANNES: I'm going to wipe that smile off your face, you little monkey! (*Na'bu just keeps on smiling.*) I don't see anything funny (*begins attacking Na'bu again—jump, kick, punch, kick, block, block, duck, duck, roundhouse kick, flip, flip, flip*).

PRINCESS KI'SHARGAL: I can see my father, he's over there!

AN'KIJ: Right! Stay with me. Let's go.

PRINCESS KI'SHAR: I will not let you win, Nin'Harsag!

NIN'HARSAG: Are you sure about that, Ki'shar?

PRINCESS KI'SHAR: I'm sure of it! (*Swing, swing, swing, kick, punch, kick, swing, swing, swing.*)

KINGU: I will fight until the end, Nunu!

LORD NUNU: Then you will die! (*Picks up Kingu and throws him across the field.*)

As Kingu gives everything he has to get back up on his feet, a hand appears from nowhere.

Voice: I'm here now, my friend.

NARRATOR: Kingu does not know who is talking and helping him to his feet. To his surprise, when he opens his eyes to thank whomever is helping him, before him, he sees it is Leo.

KINGU: Did you bring me something back? (*Passes out.*)

LEO: Rest now, my friend (*as he lay Kingu down with a smile on his face*).

LORD NUNU: Leo!

GAGA: It's Leo.

E'NURN: It really is him! (*Laughs.*)

PRINCESS KI'SHAR: Leo! He won't save you said Nin'harsag.

O'ANNES: It's Leo. About time you got here!

NANNOUR: Father, you're back!

LEO: Yes, and everything will be fine now! (*Naf'mu flies down.*) Are you really…?

NAF'MU: Yes, this will be fun!

LEO: Right! This one is mine, so stay out of my way. (*While still in* his second form.)

NAF'MU, *laughing*: Right! (*He takes off flying, cutting down everyone he passes by, many of which he took up and some time later, they came down on their own.*)

LEO: Attack!

LORD NUNU: Come, Leo!

FI'KUN: He mustn't be freed!

PRINCE A'NU: I'll be the judge of that.

FI'KUN: No! You don't know what you're doing by freeing him. He will destroy us all.

BA'LAR: Enough of this, Prince.

FI'KUN: You will all be destroyed!

PRINCE A'NU: Make it quick, Ba'lar.

BA'LAR: Yes, my prince! (*He puts the final blow to Fi'kun's head, killing him.*)

PRINCE A'NU: Ma'habi!

MA'HABI: Yes, my prince.

PRINCE A'NU: So this is where he's at?

MA'HABI: Yes, he's below us. I can feel him.

PRINCE A'NU: Give me your powers! (*They all close their eyes and give their powers to Prince A'nu, and then he begins to burst through the rocks where Ninsish'zidda was trapped many, many seasons ago. Boom, boom, boom, boom, boom! Then the rocks of the mountain caves in.*)

KIN'SI KAAH: You did it!

PRINCE A'NU: Is there anyone down there?

MA'HABI: Can you see anything?

PRINCE A'NU: No! Is there anyone down there? (*And still, not a word is said.*)

BA'LAR: Maybe there's nothing down there.

PRINCE A'NU: I'm going down there to see for myself.

AN'LB: No, Prince, what if something happens?

MA'HABI: Yes, he's right, my prince, don't go down there!

PRINCE A'NU: I didn't come all this way for nothing! I'm going down there, just stay here. (*He jumps down into the darkness of the cave, and the only light is from the hole he had just made.*)

LORD NUNU: It's about time you showed up, you coward! (*Swing, swing, block, block, the sounds of their swords clashing, kick, block, punch, punch, block, block.*)

LEO: Why are you doing this, Nunu? (*Punch, punch, kick, kick, flip, flip, duck, block, block, jump, kick, duck, block.*)

LORD NUNU: Why, you say? Why, you say? Don't give me that, you murderer! (*Kick, block, punch, flip, flip, jump, swing, swing, sounds of swords continuing to clash, but Leo doesn't know what is going on or why they are at war.*)

LEO: Murderer? Why do you call me a murderer, Nunu? (*Punch, kick, swing, swing, swing.*)

LORD NUNU: Don't give me that! You know what you've done. You killed my son! I've trusted you, cats, and this is how you repay me? (*Kick, block, punch, block, swing, block, flip, flip, swing, block, duck, jump, swing, block, the scent of a cat on his body.*) You liar!

LEO: You've got it all wrong, Nunu. I didn't kill your son, and no one from my pride killed your son. There must be an answer to all this! (*Swing, swing, block, jump, flip, flip, duck, kick—all the while, their swords steadily clashing.*)

LORD NUNU: I'll tell you the answer: when your whole pride is dead, Leo! (*Swing, swing, punch, kick, punch, block, block, kick.*)

NARRATOR: As Prince A'nu lands at the bottom of the cave, the only light he has is coming from the hole he had made coming in. He stands in the middle of the light.

PRINCE A'NU: Is anyone there? (*He could hear the sounds of chains moving all around him.*) Who's there?

NINSISH'ZIDDA: Who are you?

PRINCE A'NU: I'm Prince A'nu!

NINSISH'ZIDDA: Prince A'nu?

PRINCE A'NU: Yes!

NINSISH'ZIDDA: (*Laughing.*)

PRINCE A'NU: Who are you?

NINSISH'ZIDDA: My name is Ninsish'zidda!

PRINCE A'NU: Ninsish'zidda, how many seasons have you been locked up in here?

NINSISH'ZIDDA: I don't know how long it's been!

PRINCE A'NU: Well, I came here to set you free because I need your help.

NINSISH'ZIDDA: Why should I help you? (*His chains could be heard moving around in the darkness, but he himself is unseen to Prince A'nu.*)

PRINCE A'NU: I want you to help me get my revenge on the pride who killed my father, that's why I'm here to release you and set you free.

NINSISH'ZIDDA: (*Laughing, sounds of his chains moving around.*)

ELEVEN: Leo is stronger now. I can feel his power from here!

QUEEN FATIMA: Yes, he is, my son is now a king, King Leo! (*With a proud, promising smile on her face, thinking about him in his earlier days. Thinking about how she has watched him grow from a child to the man that stands before her today, out in the field. The man that's rightfully taken his place of leadership as a purebred king, defending his pride as only a true king could. Seeing now that he's become the man and king that his father, King Lee, would be proud of, makes the queen's smile grow more broader and wider, just relishing in the thought of the king they've raised.*) Thinking aloud—But at the end of the day, it's King Leo's pride.

DAU'RU: We will win this war now!

ELEVEN: Yes, Dau'ru we will win! (With them looking down at the battlefield from the lookout, seeing that Leo's return is giving them the fighting chance that they needed.

VOICE: Hello…

QUEEN FATIMA: Who said that?

ELEVEN: I don't know, my queen, but it looks like someone else is coming!

DAU'RU: It looks like Ni'nib. Yes, it is her, but who's that she's got with her? (*As she gets closer and closer at top speed.*)

NI'NIB, *yelling up to the lookout point*: I found him Now where's Leo?

QUEEN FATIMA: Hurry! They're in the field, Ni'nib, you must get there fast.

NI'NIB: Will do, hold on, Fon'du (*running with everything she's got, trying to make it there in time*).

NA'BU: (*Ancient monkey talk*)

O'ANNES: Quit smiling! (*He swings, but misses, then kicks, but he moves out of the way.*) Stop that!

NA'BU: (*Ancient monkey talk.*) (*With a kick, flip, punch, duck, swing, punch, punch, his sword knocks O'annes maul hammer out of his hand, then hits him repeatedly.*)

KING LEO: Lord Nunu, why are you doing this? You and my father made peace long ago, so why this? (*Flip, duck, block, kick, swing, swing, swing.*)

LORD NUNU: How dare you say the word *peace* after killing my son! (*Swing, swing, swing, block, block, kick, punch, punch, kick.*)

PRINCESS KI'SHARGAL: Father, Father! (*Now finally reaching him, as he fights with Leo.*)

LORD NUNU: Stand aside, my child, because this murderer has to pay for what he's done!

PRINCESS KI'SHARGAL: No, Father! (*As Lord Nunu pushes her out his way to continue his fight with Leo. Swing, swing, swing, block, block, duck, duck, flip, flip, flip, punch, punch, punch.*) Do something (*she tells An'kij*)!

AN'KIJ: We must stay out of it, Ki'shargal.

PRINCESS KI'SHARGAL: No! This is wrong, An'kij!

As she watches her father and Leo fight, a voice from nowhere yells out loud.

VOICE: Leo!

GAGA: It's Ni'nib. She finally made it!

NI'NIB: Leo! (*She runs up to him, fighting with Lord Nunu.*)

LEO: What is it, Ni'nib? You have to move.

NI'NIB: You have to stop this, Leo, you and Lord Nunu. I know who started this war, and I found who saw them!

PRINCESS KI'SHARGAL: What are you talking about? (*Hearing Ni'nib saying she knows who killed her brother.*)

NI'NIB: Yes, I know who killed your brother, and he's the one who saw him killed!

PRINCESS KI'SHARGAL: He did! Tell me who killed my brother. (*She grabs hold of him.*)

NI'NIB: He told me that it was Prince A'nu!

PRINCESS KI'SHARGAL: Prince A'nu!

NI'NIB: Yes, he knows everything.

PRINCESS KI'SHARGAL: You're right! (*Looking at Ni'nib dead in her eyes, she turns and yells*) Father, you must stop this at once! (*As he releases him, she runs to her father.*)

LORD NUNU: I don't have time for this, Ki'shargal! (*As he avoids her and keeps on with his attacks on Leo. Swing, swing, swing, kick, kick, punch, kick, block, duck, block, duck, flip, flip, and into the air they go and back down again, making a small crater.*)

PRINCESS KI'SHARGAL: Stop, Father, please! It wasn't the pride who killed Zwolle, it was Prince A'nu who did it, not Leo, Father. He lied to us. Please stop this! (*With the love in his daughter's voice, Lord Nunu stopped and turned to her and said.*)

LORD NUNU: Yes, my child, I hear you! (*He stops his fight with Leo.*) Who'd you say killed your brother?

PRINCESS KI'SHARGAL: It was A'nu, Father, he lied to us!

LORD NUNU: How do you know this, Ki'shargal?

PRINCESS KI'SHARGAL: He knows everything! (*She turns and points at Fon'du.*) Now tell my father the same thing that you told me.

LORD NUNU: Now tell me what you know of this matter, creature, or I will drink from your skull (*as he walks up to Fon'du*)!

NI'NIB: It's Okay, don't be afraid, just tell him what you told me, all right. Everything's fine (*looking at him to let him know that he's still safe with her*).

FON'DU: Right! (*He smiles back at her, and then he starts telling the things that took place up to him being a witness to his son's killing.*) Well, they were talking about something, but I was too far. So I got closer to see who it was and what they were talking about. Just between me and you, don't no one come out there that far. But, yes, they did and when I got closer to see who they were, that's when they started attacking him, but the first two wasn't a match for him. It was the hyena who killed him and put something on his body. I didn't see what it was because they heard me, and that's when they chased me.

LORD NUNU: You liar! How dare you tell me that! A'nu was the one who brought me his body and told me that it was the pride who did it, and he saw them do it.

FON'DU: No! I saw them do it. Please don't kill me. He is the one who is lying!

LORD NUNU: Die, you liar!

LEO: Wait! Lord Nunu, let's just say what you are saying is true, how do you know that it was one of us besides what A'nu told you?

PRINCESS KI'SHARGAL: Yes, Father, Leo's right. How do we really know that it was one of them?

LORD NUNU: I'll tell you how! The scent of a cat was all over his body, and I found this in my son's hand! (*He shows them the peace of cloth from Ni'nib's armor.*)

NI'NIB: That's mine, Leo!

LEO: How is it yours, Ni'nib?

NI'NIB: Look, it's from me! (*She shows them the missing piece of her armor.*) See, he took it, the one I fought when they attacked the herds, that's how he got the scent.

LEO: I remember now, Ni'nib, you're right!

PRINCESS KI'SHARGAL: Father, what now?

But her father couldn't say a word, thinking about how he'd been tricked and betrayed by the one who really killed his son.

LEO: Where is A'nu now?

PRINCESS KI'SHARGAL: Father!

LORD NUNU: Yes, my child, I'm here. I don't know where he's at, but please forgive me Leo for this. I just didn't see this coming! (*He turns and makes a loud monkey roar, which makes every monkey with a weapon stop fighting.*)

MAR'DUK: What's going on?

E'NANMA: I don't know!

NINUR'TA: Something is wrong. We will finish this! (*She takes off.*)

PRINCESS KI'SHAR: Yes, we will! (*She watches her fly off.*)

NA'BU: Ancient monkey talk!

O'ANNES: Come on now, you can't leave. I was just about to get started! (*Both of his eyes closed.*) Now you go now, before I change my mind. (*Smiles.*)

E'NANMA: Lord Nunu, what's the meaning of this? (*Everyone walks up to him.*)

LORD NUNU: I've been tricked, my friends!

MAR'DUK: Now I'll fade one to that! (*He takes a swig from his bo'ta.*)

E'NANMA: Tricked?

LORD NUNU: Yes!

NINUR'TA: Do tell?

LORD NUNU: The pride wasn't the ones who killed him.

E'NANMA: If it wasn't the pride, who then, Lord Nunu?

LORD NUNU: A'nu!

NINUR'TA: Do you know what this means?

LORD NUNU: Yes.

NINUR'TA: The laws of this land have been broken!

E'NANMA: He must pay for this with his life!

LEO: You're right, with his life, he shall!

NAF'MU: (*He lands in front of Leo, after taking another one for a long ride up.*) What is it, my friend?

LEO: Naf'mu, my friend, the laws have been broken, and we have a special someone in mind! (*He transforms back to his first form.*)

PRINCE A'NU: So what's it going to be? Are you going to help me or not because you can stay in here for all seasons to come. Last chance!

And with that said, the sounds of the chains stopped, and before Prince A'nu could say another word, leaping off his head he went, and out the cave Ninsish'zidda goes.

BA'LAR: Hi! Who are you, and where's Prince A'nu?

Ninsish'zidda just looks at him with a smile on his face.

AN'LB: You heard him! Where's Prince A'nu?

NARRATOR: Before they got ready to attack him, Ninsish'zidda looks up at the light of the sun, and then there's a roar that hadn't been heard since the founding of any of the kingdoms. Then he burst into flames, the heat from his power making them sweat.

KIN'SIKAAH: What is he!

MA'HABI: This is very bad!

BA'LAR: I'm not going to ask you why you said that.

MA'HABI: His power is pure evil! I don't know what we've done, but I don't think that we should've let him out!

NARRATOR: They look up at Ninsish'zidda, who is making this very loud, deep rumbling sound. And every tree that is on top of mountains are set unto flames, and the smoke reaches for miles up into the heavens. All who had eyes can see it.

Lord Nunu: (*He turns to see the mountain with a look on his face.*) This can't be!

Everyone turns around to see what's making that deep loud roar.

Leo: What's making that sound, Nunu?

But Nunu isn't answering him. His mouth hangs open and his eyes are looking to a far, far away place—the mountain!

Ni'nib: What's making that noise so loud?

Ninur'ta: We're all doomed! (*Everyone looks toward the mountain.*)

Queen Fatima: Why are the mountains on fire like that, and what's making that noise?

Eleven: I don't know, my queen, but whatever it is, watching it from here, it doesn't look good! (*They continue watching from the lookout.*)

Ha'kim: This world as we know it is over now that he's free! (*Thinking to himself,* Now that the past has returned.)

EN'LILS: Our master has returned to us! (*All the evils of the forest are now free to come out and play, their sounds of laughter coming from the darkness.*)

QUEEN GU'DET: He's coming for us all! (*She sits in her room, looking out at the smoke-filled mountains.*)

NINSISH'ZIDDA: (*Roooaaarrr!*)

TBC

About the Author

Readers will be interested in this art and story simply because it's something new, something that hasn't been told from this point of view. He takes you to a world before humans—a world where animals ruled and reached a superior level of evolving with human characteristics and traits.

About the Book

"But at the end of the day…" lies, deception, envy, and greed have plagued this world. Even as far back as the Mesozoic Era, before dinosaurs, you had the Permian Era—an era that brought about the synapsid (reptiles with waterproof skin) hybrids and many more unique colonized creatures. You had the clan of unique and powerful cats and the disastrous clan of hyenas, monkey tribes, etc. These creatures were humanlike in every way, from being compassionate to cunning, brilliant to dim-witted, many very conniving and treacherous (just like many today). They were tempted by power and they will to do anything to gain it, even kill.

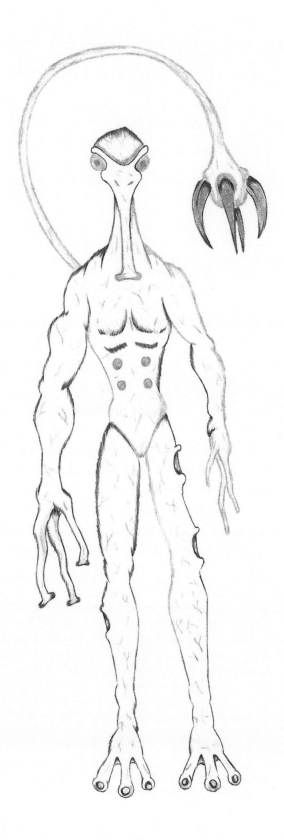

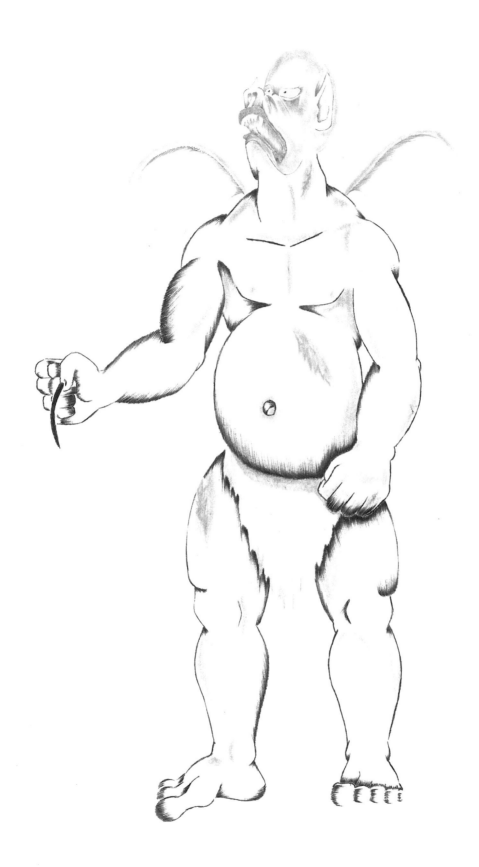

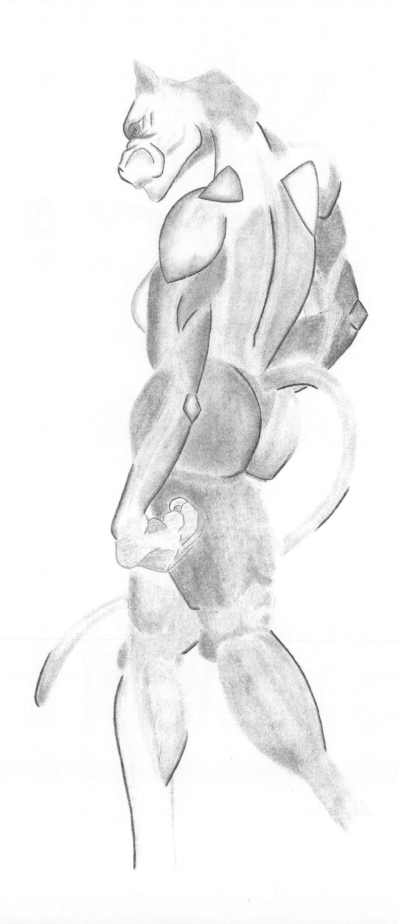

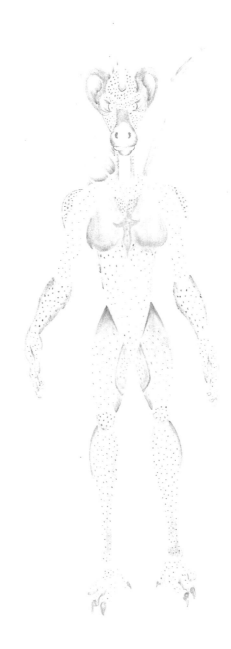

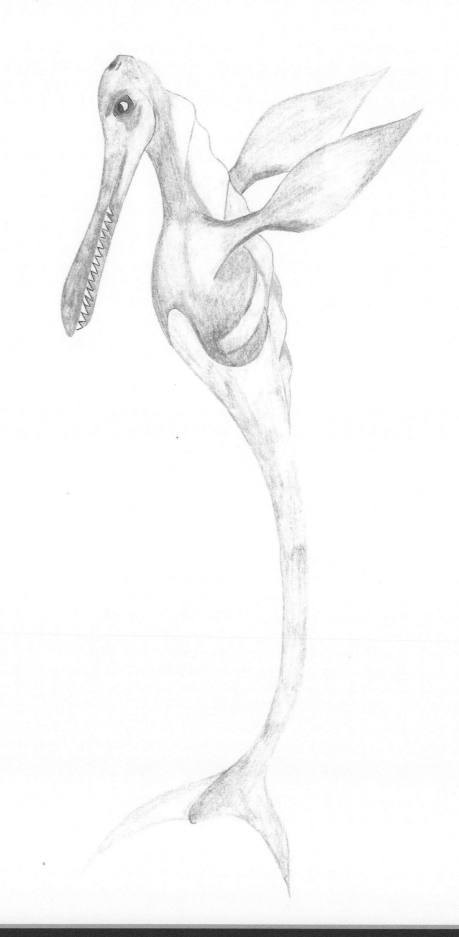

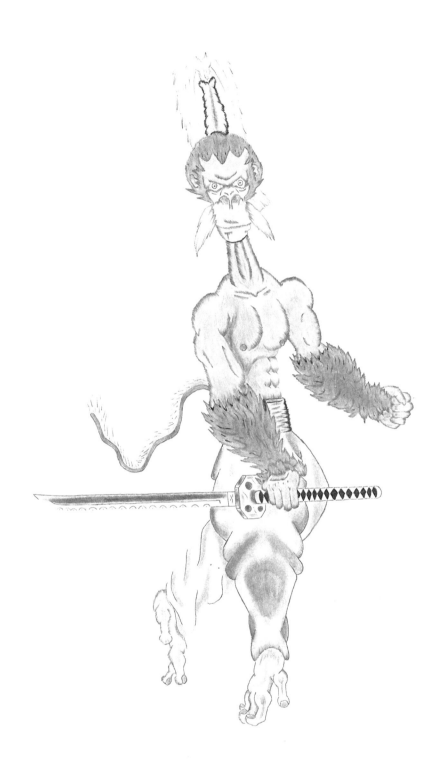

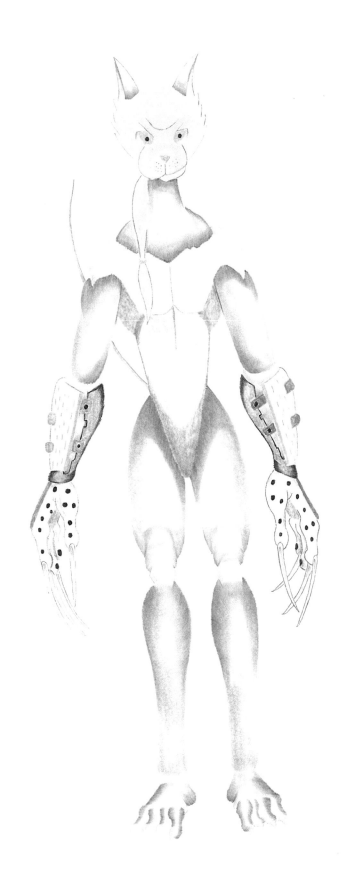

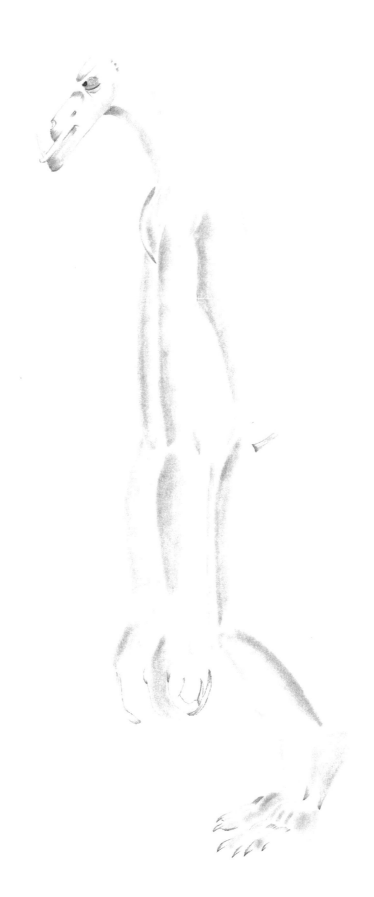

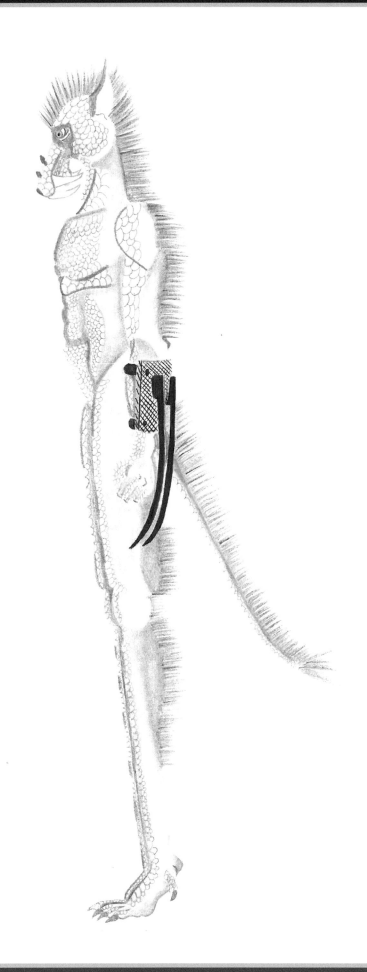

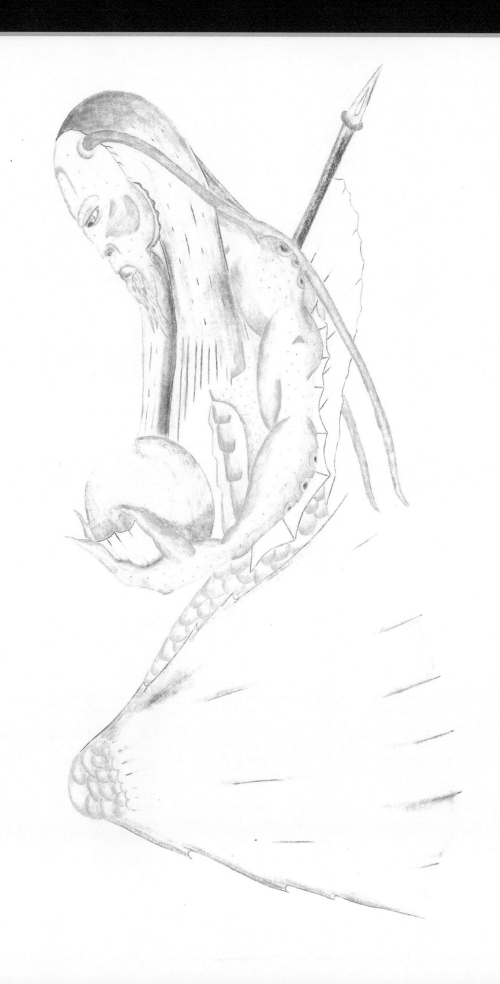

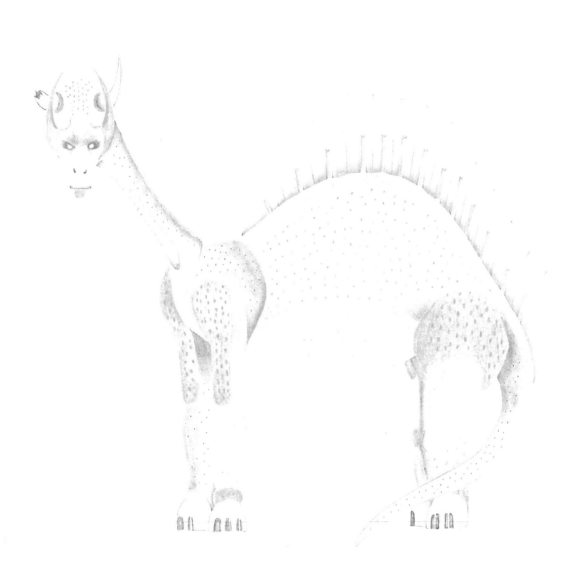

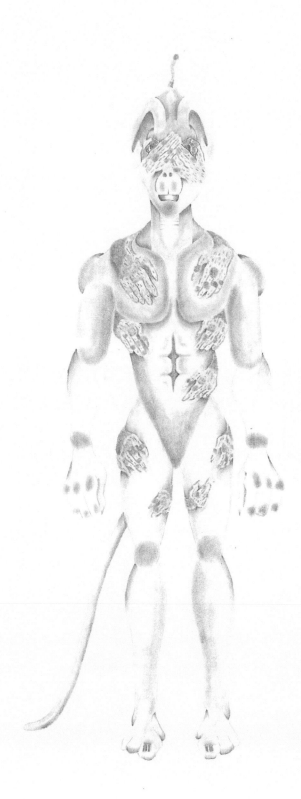

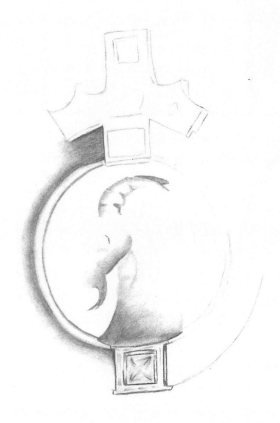

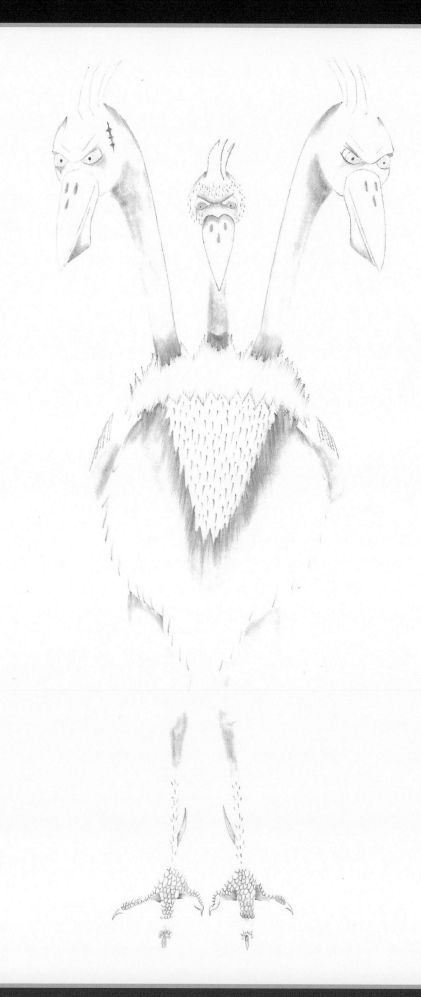

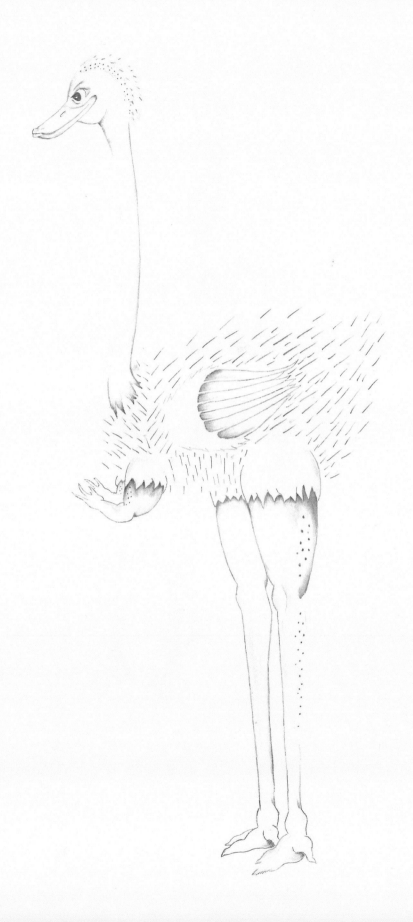

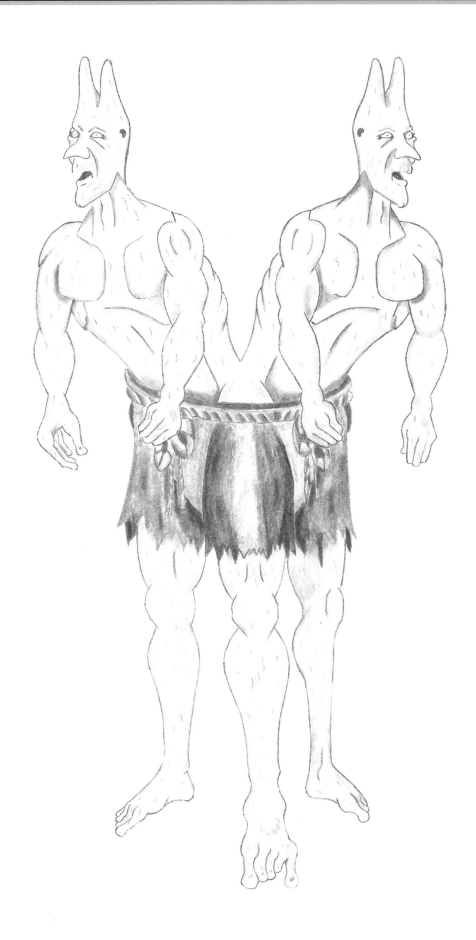

Printed in the United States
By Bookmasters